"Would you prefer [...] someone else present?"

"I understand how it might not seem appropriate for you to be alone with an outsider so soon after…" *Your husband's death*, John was going to say, but decided that would be callous and just allowed his sentence to drift off and for her to come to her own conclusion.

"I think that would be better, Mr. Fisher. My sister is visiting me early evening. Would it be possible for you to return at seven?"

"Of course, Mrs. Miller. I understand how difficult this must be for you."

Emma nodded and smiled.

John couldn't help but smile back. He turned and was about to step off the porch to return to his car, but he stopped and took a minute to take in the view. "This place just doesn't change, does it?" he said, not really directing the question at Emma.

"You've been here before?"

"Oh, yes, Mrs. Miller, I've been here before," John said, turning to face the pretty young widow again. "I used to live here."

Hannah Schrock is the bestselling author of numerous Amish romance and Amish mystery books.

AMISH ANGUISH

Hannah Schrock

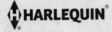

ISBN-13: 978-1-335-48499-4

Amish Anguish

First published in 2015 by Burton Crown Ltd.
This edition published in 2021.

Recycling programs
for this product may
not exist in your area.

This edition published by arrangement with Harlequin Books S.A.

For questions and comments about the quality of this book, please contact us at CustomerService@Harlequin.com.

Harlequin Enterprises ULC
22 Adelaide St. West, 40th Floor
Toronto, Ontario M5H 4E3, Canada
www.Harlequin.com

Printed in U.S.A.

AMISH ANGUISH

Prologue

An Unwelcome Proposal

"You want me to get married to a man I don't even know?" Emma Byler asked with not a minimal level of shock as she met her mother's firm gaze.

"Of course you know him; you've seen them at church." Bethany Byler had a way of making the most significant factors sound insignificant. The way her eyes bored into Emma, made her feel small and foolish for even questioning her mother's suggestion.

"What about Ruth? She is the eldest; she should be the one who gets married first. I'm only twenty-two, and he is already somewhere in his thirties, I suppose. *Mamm*, surely you can't expect me to just go along with this?" Emma stood up from the kitchen table and walked to the window.

"Emma, you are being completely unreasonable. David Miller is a good *mann*, a good *mann* who has asked me for your hand in marriage. What did you expect me to do? Turn him away just so you can hang on to the dream of finding true love? There is no such thing. Most marriages start on a basis of friendship, understanding and respect. Love comes later. This is a good *mann* asking for your hand and I won't deny him."

"If he is such a good *mann*, why didn't he come to me? Why come to you?" Emma asked irritably.

She heard her sister Ruth chuckle from the corner of the room and shook her head. "What's so funny?"

"Just the fact that *Mamm* is arranging a husband for you, just like she arranged everything else for you in your life," Ruth said with a sting that held a tinge of jealousy.

"Girls, hush! Ruth, I didn't ask your opinion. Emma, I've never asked anything of you. You have always done willingly what needed to be done. For the first time in my life I'm asking you to take off the blindfold and look to your future. This *mann* can offer you a future, and in time you'll grow to love and respect him. There is no shame in having an arranged marriage. In fact if you asked around, most of the elderly people in our community are in arranged marriages, and they will freely admit that they now love their partners. This is an opportunity for you. An opportunity that doesn't come along every day. I want to hear no more about it. You're getting married in two weeks and that's that."

Bethany turned and walked out of the kitchen leaving Emma staring out the window with tears streaming down her face. She had always dreamed that one day she would fall in love and be swept off her feet by a *mann* of her dreams. Never in a million years had she imagined her mother arranging a husband for her.

Emma brushed away the tears, knowing they wouldn't help. She had always adhered to her mother's wishes, and that wouldn't change now. Although she wasn't happy with the arrangement, or that she would have no hopes of marrying the man she had been working for over the last week, she wouldn't go against her mother's decision.

Unlike her sister Ruth, who went against her mother on every aspect of her life, Emma had always been the quieter, more compassionate one of the two Byler sisters. A fact that she now regretted.

Why couldn't she be more like Ruth? Why couldn't she do as she chose? The Ten Commandments came to mind and she knew that she wouldn't be able to not honor her mother without regretting it afterward.

In two weeks' time she would walk down the aisle, she would give her vows to a man she didn't love, and until then she would pray every single night that God would guide her in her marriage. This might not be the man that she had chosen for herself, but she would do her best to be the wife he expected her to be.

Perhaps in a few months, or a few years, love would grow out of mutual respect. And perhaps in time, she would love him enough to have his children. Her heart clenched in her chest even as her tummy formed into a tight coil of nerves. At this moment, none of that seemed possible.

She turned away from the window and headed to

her room. If she was to be married in only two weeks and moving out of the family home, she had a lot to get done. But before she did anything, she would pray.

Chapter One

Emma's anguish

Emma Miller stared down at the grin on her husband David's face and wondered how it could ever have come to this.

Six months ago her life was so completely different. She had been unmarried back then and living with her mother. She was happy with her life, enjoying her favorite pastime of baking, meeting with her friends and staying for the singings after church. She had begun work as a server in a newly opened Amish restaurant. It brought some much-needed money into the household while giving her the opportunity to meet new people on an ongoing basis. Her confidence had improved markedly since taking on the job. Before that, she would never so much as have said a squeak to anyone she didn't know unless she had to. Now she was warm and welcoming and always ready to make conversation and eager to speak to anyone she met.

She had always been grateful to David for giving her the job in the first place. But that was all it was. Gratitude. She had never expected a proposal arranged by her mother only a week later.

Her mother had been keen on her match with David. Emma had to confess to having been slightly less keen on the proposed marriage and had not been afraid to tell her mother as much.

After the initial argument, Emma had asked her mother again to reconsider. But Bethany had been firm that the arrangements were already made. When Emma began to beg, her mother responded with horror stories of spinsters and missing out on marriage prospects. Her sister's name was mentioned more than once during the conversation, often coupled with phrases such as, "You don't want to end up like her." Emma had always been a dutiful daughter. If her mother believed this to be God's will, then she would go along with it. She knew that she didn't love David but hoped that love might be something that would grow with time.

Despite the fact David was almost nine years older than her, he was incredibly handsome and had just started an exciting new restaurant business, in which she was already employed. It all seemed to make sense, at least that is what her mother kept telling her. Out of the other possible matches in the community, even Emma had to admit that David was probably the best option as a husband. They could be happy.

It may have made sense, but it wasn't love. Emma had grown up dreaming of love, what little girl doesn't? And so it was with a twinge of disappointment that she had married David less than three months ago. Not because she was in love with the man of her dreams, but because her mother believed it to be the correct course of action.

The first weeks of marriage are meant to be idyllic, with the newlyweds visiting the homes of the people they know. However, tragedy soon reared its head.

Her mother, long since widowed, developed pneumonia just four days after the wedding. Her health deteriorated rapidly, and she died, giving herself up to God's calling, relieved that she had at least seen one daughter safely married. Emma gained some comfort from the fact that she'd acted on her mother's wishes and married the man of her choosing. Her mother must have had some peace and reassurance from that. Emma was also glad that she had the security offered by her new husband. After all, he was the owner of a prosperous, exciting business.

But of course, that wasn't strictly speaking the case.

The new business wasn't quite as exciting as she had been led to believe. The restaurant building itself wasn't owned by David but leased. The refurbishments that David had authorized before he opened the doors to the paying public had all been paid for with large loans extended recklessly by *Englisch* banks. The takings received from the restaurant were barely enough to service the debt each month. The meagre amount of money Emma's mother had left her in her will was immediately swallowed up and given to the banks to pay off a proportion of the debt. The debt at least was manageable now, but the newly married couple were hardly bringing enough home to pay the rent on the little house in which they lived. It was a desperate situation. Emma had taken to selling her quilts to an *Englisch* woman in town who then resold them on the internet. But quilting took time and it wasn't a sensible long-term answer to rescue them out of their difficulties. They needed a positive option and quickly.

She looked down at the placid expression on David's face and she wanted to shake him awake and demand his reasons for not having told her all this before they actually got married. She wanted answers and she wanted an apology.

But of course she couldn't shake David awake.

Because David was dead.

After only ninety-six days of marriage.

In the last three months she had experienced more than most did at double her age. She had been married, lost her last remaining parent, rendering her an orphan, and become a widow. On top of all that she was left with a restaurant business that was heavily in debt and lived in a house on which the rent was due in less than a fortnight.

Ninety-six days.

Emma didn't know what on Earth had hit her or why God had chosen her to endure this unspeakable anguish.

The door opened silently behind her and someone slipped into the back of the room.

"It's time," the voice whispered gently.

Emma turned and saw her sister Ruth standing quietly in the back. Emma nodded at her. She and Ruth had never been that close. More than once Ruth had flirted with the idea of leaving the Amish community, but each time she was persuaded against it by their mother. With her mother now gone Emma believed it wouldn't be long before Ruth left.

"Was that the policeman back again earlier?" Emma asked, gazing once again at her dead husband's face.

"Yes," Ruth admitted. "I was hoping you didn't hear. I told him that he had to come back another time. I mean, turning up on the day of the funeral. Didn't the fifty buggies outside give the *mann* some clue?"

Ruth was very good at speaking her mind, and sometimes her mouth moved before her brain had time to catch up. As a result, many people in the community didn't warm to her, and Emma felt that this would only help to push Ruth away even quicker. Ruth was two years older than Emma, but Emma always had the impression that Ruth's Rumspringa had never quite seen its end! Emma had to however give credit where it was due; Ruth had certainly rallied round her these last few days and helped to organize all that needed to be done. She strongly doubted that she would have been able to do anything on her own without her sister's help.

"Did he say anything new?" Emma asked.

"No, no more than we know already," Ruth replied. "They're still making inquiries at the local gas stations and businesses. Nothing new has come up."

"I don't think we'll ever find out what happened," Emma said, shaking her head, still in disbelief at the entire situation.

"They'll find them. The police are very good at this sort of thing. They found fragments of the paint on the buggy. I believe that they can get these samples tested in laboratories and be able to match it to a specific vehicle. Whoever did this won't be able to hide forever."

Emma was amazed at Ruth's knowledge of the outside world. Who would have thought that the police would be able to test paint fragments and use them to apprehend whoever had done this to her husband? It was a truly wondrous ability.

"The policeman did say that they managed to do a preliminary test on the buggy," Ruth continued. "He said there didn't seem to be any mechanical issues there. I mean, there wouldn't be though, would there? It's just a simple buggy. So unless the horse bolted, David certainly could not have been at fault."

Suddenly Emma remembered that not only had David been killed, their beautiful horse, Sampson, had succumbed in the tragedy as well. She began worrying about how she would get to the restaurant without the means of a buggy or a horse. It was all simply becoming too much for her.

"I think we can safely assume that David wasn't at fault at all. Otherwise the driver of the vehicle involved would have stopped, surely?" Emma replied with an air of despondency.

The policeman had told her that David had been driving home from the restaurant as normal. It appeared that something had run his buggy off the road. From the witness reports, it definitely seemed as if the car had intentionally pushed the horse-drawn buggy off the road.

Another road user had stopped and telephoned for

help on a cell phone, but by then it was already too late. The responsible person hadn't stopped at the scene, raising suspicions of a hit and run among both Emma and the police. The more she thought about it the more wrong it sounded. It had happened on a clear day with no signs of rain and no fog. With good visibility in the middle of the day, it simply didn't make sense.

But then, Emma admitted to herself, not much in her life had made sense since she agreed to marry David.

"I'm just thankful that you weren't in the buggy as well, Emma," said Ruth, coming forward and gently laying her hands on her sister's shoulders. "It would have been too much to lose you as well, after everything else these last few weeks."

Emma turned and smiled at her sister. It was true; Emma would typically have been with David in the buggy. On the day in question, however, she had felt unwell and she hadn't made the trip to the restaurant. David said that it was probably all due to the worry and upset of losing her mother, and that she should take a few days off to rest and recuperate. But now Emma felt guilty. David was only late leaving the restaurant that evening because Emma wasn't there to help out; they couldn't afford any relief staff to step in and help.

"*Jah*, but if I was, we would have left the restaurant on time and David wouldn't have been on the road at the time that the vehicle had been to run him and Sampson off the road. It is my fault!"

"Hush, little *schweschder*," said Ruth, pulling her close. "You can't go on thinking like that. The chances are that the buggy would still have been hit and you would be lying beside David right now. Or best-case scenario, you would be holed up in a hospital room, receiving treatment for your injuries"

"*Denke*, Ruth," Emma said, burying her head in her sister's neck. "I don't know how I'm going to cope. I mean, I haven't told you this before, but it seems that David's business wasn't as prosperous as our mother had assumed."

"Calm down," said Ruth. "Now isn't the time to talk of such matters." She moved over to look at her brother-in-law, peaceful in death. "Let's get today over and done with and then we can talk and come up with a plan."

There was a discreet knock at the door. Ruth dried Emma's eyes with her own handkerchief. "Are you ready?"

Emma took a very deep breath and nodded. She stood back as six men entered the house. They closed the coffin before carrying it out to the buggy that was to take David to the cemetery. Emma could feel emotion plugging her throat. Not because she grieved over the loss of her husband, but because of the situation she now found herself in.

David had been nothing but kind to her since their wedding day, but she had yet to grow to love him. She was a widow at the age of twenty-two and had no idea how she was going to climb out of the hole her marriage to David had left her in.

Chapter Two

The Englisch lawyer

John Fisher removed his reading glasses and rubbed his eyes with the heels of his hands. They stung. He looked up at the clock to see that it was 5:15. It was little wonder that his eyes stung; he had been staring at paperwork for more than twelve hours. He probably needed a break. To be honest, he probably needed to go home and sleep for about a week, but there was little chance of that happening.

Ever since his first day on the job he had always made a habit of being the first person in the office. As a teenager growing up, he had diligently read every novel released by John Grisham. His favorite was still his first, *The Firm*. It had inspired him to become a lawyer in the first place. In fact, he had read the book so many times that the cover had come away. In his first year in his own firm he would still pretend to be Mitch McDeere, beating all the others in the office and very nearly working himself into the grave in the process.

His secretary, Carol, glided into his office, with her red hair, scarlet lips and a mid-length tight fitting skirt. She was almost forty but she looked thirty and had a smile that lit up the room whenever she walked in.

"Right, John. That's me done for the day," she said with a notepad and pen in her hand in case any last second instructions were fired at her. "Mr. Seymour has just been on the phone, he wants you to nip upstairs before you go home. He apparently wants to discuss something with you."

"No worries," replied John. "At least it will get me away from this never-ending river of papers."

"Is there anything else you need from me before I go?" asked Carol, making it exceedingly apparent that she was hoping there wouldn't be.

"No," said John with a grin. "You go home and enjoy your evening. Zumba night, isn't it?"

"Oh yes," Carol said, with a shake of her hips.

"Lucky instructor!"

Carol grinned at the compliment and turned for the office door, when John shouted after her. "Friday tomorrow. Donut day. Don't forget!"

"How could I? This place does nothing for my figure," she jokingly grumbled as she practically ran out of the office.

John stood up and his right knee creaked under the strain. It had never been right since the two-hundred-and-seventy-five-pound linebacker put his shoulder through it at college. Sitting in one position for too long always made the injury play up. He stretched and looked in the mirror that was meant to give his office the illusion of size. He was twenty seven and was beginning to look his age. If he let his hair grow too long, little flecks of gray would appear. That's what three years of practicing law will do to you, he thought. Of course, most of the secretaries thought something completely different.

Despite the flecks of gray, John Fisher was a handsome man, six foot six and well built. The only reason he was still single was that he spent eighteen hours a day in the offices of Seymour and Pascal, Attorneys at Law. He never went anywhere to meet anyone with whom to enjoy any measure of a romantic attachment.

He grabbed his jacket from the back of the door and slipped it on. He straightened his tie and nodded to himself in the mirror. It always paid to make sure you looked the part before visiting the managing partner. The last thing Seymour would want to see was a tired, worn out and haggard associate. Especially if the topic of the meeting turned out to be as he suspected. He turned away from the elevator and took the two flights of stairs two at a time to make sure he was fully awake. Karl Seymour's two secretaries were still hard at work; they smiled warmly at John when he came in.

"Good afternoon, Mr. Fisher, he says you are to go straight in," Juliet the elder of the two said, indicating the door.

"Thanks, Juliet," replied John. "Can I say, you are looking lovelier than ever."

"Get out of it!" shot back Juliet, who was old enough to be his mother.

John grinned and winked at the young blonde, Debbie, before knocking quickly on Seymour's door and opening without bothering to wait for a reply.

Seymour's office was somewhat more palatial than John's own. It was a corner office and two of the four walls were ceiling-to-floor glass, which afforded a great view of the city and the lake below. His was one of those old-fashioned partner desks with a shiny oak top and brilliant brass handles. Seymour claimed it was a genuine antique, something to do with Lord Nelson's ship, Victory, constructed of timber damaged at Trafalgar. It was a beautiful piece of furniture, but no one believed a word of the back story. The iMac positioned upon it looked a little out of place, to be honest.

Karl Seymour was seated on his black leather Chesterfield couch, his blue tie loosened and a large glass of Scotch on the rocks in his hand.

"Ah, here he is," he said in his English accent. Seymour had moved to the United States from Kent, the Garden of England, when he was seventeen. His father was some hotshot in the oil industry, and he traveled the world on a regular basis. Karl liked the country so much that he attended a local college before going on to law school. He never returned home to the British Isles.

"Sit down, John," said Seymour, indicating the couch opposite his own. John obeyed and found himself facing the partner's ego wall displaying the certificates, diplomas and newspaper cuttings of famous courtroom victories. Amongst the affirmations was a framed picture of himself with President Clinton. Lawyers knew how to highlight their status.

"Do you want a drink, John?" a voice asked from the adjoining conference room. A bald head appeared from around the door frame, quickly followed by a hand waving a whiskey glass in the air.

The bald head belonged to Pierre Pascal, the other partner in this money printing firm. Pascal was the grandson of a French immigrant, and he never let anyone forget his European roots, regularly debating France's superiority to Great Britain with his partner. Of course, other than his name there was nothing French about Pascal. A proper Frenchman would drink fine red wines and eat patè and blue steak for dinner. Pascal, on the other hand, drank beer and bourbon, sometimes at the same time, and as his waistline confirmed his preference for pizza over fine French cuisine.

"No, sir, I'm good, thank you."

"Good to hear, drinking in the office is a terrible idea," replied Pascal, emerging with a large straight-up bourbon. He slumped into the couch at the opposite end to John.

"So, John," began Seymour. "You know we have this trial coming up."

Of course John knew about the trial. Everyone in the Midwest knew about the trial. The drug dealing teacher who had arranged a hit on a student who had failed to pay what he owed. At least, that is what the government said. In two months, Karl Seymour was going to stand up in court and attest to the poor man being completely innocent and without a blemish on his character.

"Of course," replied John expectantly. He had been laying the ground work for months and he wanted to be in on the trial. Obviously Karl Seymour would be the lead counsel, but John felt that there was probably a place at the table, albeit the far end of the table, for a hard-working young associate.

"You know I need the best people helping me on this, and I want you to be part of the team," continued Seymour.

John grinned from ear to ear. This would be his first experience of big-time courtroom action. "Sir, I will make you proud."

Seymour nodded his appreciation, "I have little doubt that you will, that's why you have been asked. Come Monday, we will have our first team meeting, 7:00 a.m. sharp. I know you will already have put a shift in before then but be switched on. I can't afford any slackers on this."

"Yes, sir, you can count on me," insisted John, eager to get started.

"But before the trial, we have a little problem," interjected Pascal, taking a gulp of his drink. "And we think you are uniquely placed in the firm to resolve it."

"How can I help, sir?" replied John, eager to please after being awarded this shot at the big time.

Pascal pointed to a rather thin looking file on the coffee table. "That there is the problem."

It didn't seem to be much of a problem to John, a file that thin couldn't take much resolving. "Okay, what is it?"

"It's a Malcolm Kennedy mistake, is what it is,"

blurted Seymour, glaring at Pascal. Kennedy was the firm's newest associate, having passed the bar exam only four months ago. John had heard rumors around the office that Seymour was never in favor of hiring him, but Pascal had got his way.

Pascal raised his hand at Seymour in silent acknowledgment that he might actually be right.

"Anyway, eleven days ago a new client walked into the building and said he wanted to draw up a new will. He wanted it done there and then as his personal circumstances had changed. A bit of background was obtained, and it was hardly a complex matter, so Kennedy was dragged down from his office to draw up the document. The client wanted to leave the majority of his earthly possessions to his wife, and a farm to his sister." Pascal bent over and picked up the file, handing it to John. "Take a look."

John opened the file and pulled out a copy of the completed will. He scanned it quickly with his lawyer eyes. It was all witnessed and signed correctly, no problems there. Pascal was right, the will listed the client's intention to bequeath a farm and four properties in Pennsylvania together with their respective incomes to his wife. It went on to list a farm in Missouri which he had willed to his sister, and what appeared to be a restaurant to his wife. Clearly this was a nice little estate but nothing out of the ordinary, and certainly a good deal smaller than most estates which the firm handled. John flicked the pages looking for something, but he failed to find it.

He looked at Pascal. "The will highlights these properties, but there is no detail on them."

"Exactly," backed up Seymour.

"Kennedy said the client was in a terrible rush and that he had claimed to have forgotten to bring the documents with him. He said he would return in a week with all of the details, but he insisted the document be drawn up in the meantime there and then so that he could sign. He was newly married, and he didn't want there to be any complications if anything should happen to him in the interim."

It wasn't the normal way you to handle a will. Typically it would be required to present the full details before any document was signed, thought John. But it was certainly a valid legal document. "So what's the problem?"

"Something did happen to him. He was killed in a hit and run two days after this document was signed," Pascal replied. "We only know this because he had our business card on him at the time, and police were in touch to find out what we knew about him."

"We need this sorted out. The client didn't take a copy of the will with him. We'd like you to take a copy to his widow and hope that she knows where the documents are that relate to these mystery properties," said Pascal.

"If she doesn't, it is going to be awfully embarrassing," declared Seymour.

Okay. It certainly wasn't the finest last will and testament ever written, and professionally the document was weak. But it was hardly a matter to legitimize involving a high-flying associate lawyer billing $350 an hour.

"Wouldn't it be more appropriate for a senior paralegal to deal with this?"

"Normally I'd agree with you, John," replied Pascal, draining his drink. "But as I said at the start of the conversation, you are uniquely positioned in the firm to deal with this situation."

"How so?" asked a confused John, opening his arms as if waiting to catch the explanation.

Pascal looked at Seymour with a pause; it was obvious he was a little apprehensive of the reaction he might receive. Seymour nodded, silently telling Pascal to get it over and done with.

"Our client, David Miller, was Amish. We want you to go to Holmes County."

John drew a sharp intake of breath. Holmes County. He hadn't been there for years. Fifteen, to be exact. He honestly believed he would never go back. John's heart bounced in his chest as the memories of his childhood came rushing back. Memories of a quieter life, and happier life. He immediately recalled the farms and the rolling hills of the close-knit community in which he had grown up.

He didn't often think back to his Amish childhood, because thinking back made him remember the day he had left. The day his father walked into his room with suitcases already packed and said they were leaving. It had been the hardest day of John's life, leaving not only his own kind behind, but also his mother whom they had buried only a few months before.

"I know that focusing on your Amish past isn't something you like to do, John," said Seymour softly. "But clearly you can see that you're the obvious choice for this job."

John couldn't argue with the partner's reasoning. Had he been placed in their position, he too would choose the only associate who for the first twelve years of his life had known only the Amish of Holmes County. Until his mother died, of course. Then his father left, taking the young John with him. Cancer was the killer. It was caught far too late to do anything. John's father completely lost his faith after that. He lost everything else as well, turned into a drunk and died of liver failure during John's first year of law school. The thought of returning to Holmes County where he had enjoyed an idyllic early childhood with loving parents was for some reason very upsetting.

He hadn't been back in fifteen years, and going back now for the first time, meant facing the life he left behind without having been given any choice in the decision.

"John?" pressed Pascal. "Are you okay with this?"

John came back to the present. "Yes, sir, of course I am," he insisted, although he wasn't completely sure whether or not he was. The partners knew everything about the associates. They had a comprehensive recruitment plan. John's past was a matter that was discussed in his interview. John never lied about his Amish roots; he just didn't tend to bring them up unless he had to.

Holmes County. That was a long time ago.

"Is the offer of that drink still available?" John asked hopefully.

Pascal slapped him on the back with a broad grin, revealing yellowing teeth. "I knew you'd be a sport about it."

John attempted a grin, but it didn't reach his eyes. He wasn't being a sport as much as doing what the partner of the firm was assigning him to do. Like any other associate, John knew if he denied this request, it would reflect on him and his career for a very long time to come.

He would go to Holmes County, deal with the widow and the will, and then return to the life he had built for himself in Cleveland. Because even though he had Amish roots, they'd been uprooted and firmly planted in Cleveland, where he had built a life for himself out of nothing. A life he enjoyed, a life in which he had made a name for himself in the circles that mattered if you wanted to become a big player in the legal arena.

Chapter Three

The will

Emma had just finished drying her eyes when the knock came on the door.

It was the day after the funeral. After a long sleepless night, Emma spent the morning greeting the visitors who arrived to check on her wellbeing, offering token assurances and offers of help. They were all very kind, but none could offer what she really needed, which was money. Then she sat down to spend the afternoon quilting and to reflect on matters and decide on a course of action.

It didn't take long for the reality of her situation to dawn. She was left with a restaurant that was barely making enough money to suffice as a living, and she was living in a rented house on which she would be expected very soon to pay up the rent due. Rent that she simply did not have. Apart from Ruth, there was absolutely nobody she could possibly turn to for money.

She had no other family. The problem seemed to be that Ruth was probably in much the same situation financially. She was living in the old family home in which they had been raised, which of course was rented, just like this one. She may well still have her share of their mother's money and could probably afford to meet the rent. Maybe the solution would be to move back home with her sister. It wasn't a course of action that she really wanted to contemplate.

Despite Ruth's understanding and help over the last few days, years of conflict and disagreement while the girls were growing up was not yet water under the bridge. Emma was happy with her simple life and was always very devout, trusting God in all she did. Ruth on the other hand, was confused and keen to experiment with *Englisch* ways. Most of which Emma believed were wrong. It had led to significant disagreements in the past. All that had happened in the past proved hard to forget. But at times like this, who else did you have to turn to but your family and *Gott*?

The tears began to flow as she mulled the situation over in her mind. What made matters worse for her was that she'd only married David because it was her mother's wish. If she'd actually loved the man, she would have been more inclined to persevere with the situation she now faced. She felt that in this case, the cliché did not hold: she had not made the bed, and she was not prepared to lie in it. She wondered if God may be punishing her for marrying a man she did not love.

Marriage should be about love, she was sure of that. But wasn't God meant to be good and kind? Surely

He would not punish Emma for obeying her mother's wishes. After all, one of the Ten Commandments was to honor your mother and father. She didn't know what to do. Confusion ravished her tormented mind. Could she sell the restaurant and get out of that completely? But then again, who would buy a going concern that was so heavily indebted? Only a fool would do that, and she knew no fools.

Would she be able to get out of the lease to this house? She didn't even know where the lease documents were, let alone what they held. Emma's mind went around in circles, and finally the pressures of the previous months released themselves and the tears streamed thick and fast down her face.

After almost an hour of tears, Emma finally admonished herself to pull herself together. Crying wasn't going to help. It did serve to release a bit of the built up of pressure, though. She decided that when Ruth visited that evening as arranged ahead of time, she was going to be completely open about her financial situation. Surely something could be worked out. The restaurant could be a real success if the effort was made, if only she could get rid of the debt that was a constant drain. The sharp rap on the door brought her back to reality. Emma got up and walked over to the door expecting to be met with yet another elderly widow with a plate of offerings or a well-intentioned casserole. She was a little startled to open the door on a very handsome *Englischer* in a suit, positioned on her porch.

"Good afternoon, may I help you?" Emma asked,

looking over the *Englischer*'s shoulder at the very expensive looking motor car that was parked outside her house.

"Good afternoon," replied John Fisher who was probably more shocked than Emma. He hadn't bothered to look up David Miller's age in the file and had driven all the way from Cleveland expecting to meet a middle-aged Amish widow. He certainly wasn't expecting a beautiful woman in her twenties to receive him at the deceased's home.

For a moment he was thoroughly tongue-tied as the large hazel eyes watched him with a terrified expression. He didn't know who she might have been expecting, but clearly she wasn't awaiting any form of good news. She was at least a few inches shorter than John, with a small frame. Her skin was like the color of fresh cream and her hazel eyes were transfixing in some way.

He felt his heart skip a beat, completely caught off guard as he was by the sudden attraction he felt for the woman before him. John couldn't remember the last time a woman had taken his breath away, not to mention a client.

He shifted in place and cleared his throat, pushing the unwelcome thoughts from his mind before summoning a smile. "Excuse me, are you Mrs. Miller? Mrs. Emma Miller?"

"Yes, sir," Emma said politely but with a touch of nerves. "Who are you?"

She looked around, almost expecting to see a stream of *Englischers* make an appearance. He had to be from the bank, Emma immediately surmised. We must have defaulted on the loans!

"My name is John Fisher, Mrs. Miller. I am from the law firm of Seymour and Pascal in Cleveland," he said, recovering his professional composure, and handing over an expensive business card to prove his introductions.

An *Englisch* lawyer, thought Emma, reading the card as though it were the most interesting book in the world. The bank would probably have been better. Things must be a lot worse than she thought.

"And how can I help you, Mr. Fisher?" asked Emma, who seemed to be transfixed by her visitor's deep green eyes. He was a tall man with a large frame, his dusty brown hair cropped a little shorter than the traditional Amish style. He wore a suit and tie as well as expertly polished shoes. So unlike the plain clothes her deceased husband had worn.

"My law firm represented your husband, Mrs. Miller. Please accept my condolences over your loss."

"Denke," Emma nodded, feeling a little intimidated by the stranger and the way in which his green eyes searched hers.

"There are some important legal matters I need to discuss with you," John said in a formal tone of voice. It was never pleasant to visit family members of the recently deceased, but it did form a very necessary part of the job. John only wished not to be distracted on this particular occasion by the widow, so much so as to cause him to almost forget his reason for being in Holmes County in the first place.

"Oh, I see," Emma managed, her heart sinking. Important legal matters could only be bad news.

John immediately saw the concern pass over her beautiful face and he broke out into a smile. "I can assure you however that there is nothing to worry about, Mrs. Miller."

Emma looked at him as though he must certainly be lying, and it was very clear that she didn't really know what to do.

John looked over her shoulder. "Do you have anyone with you?"

"Umm, no. I'm afraid I don't," Emma reluctantly admitted. The man looked respectful enough, but she had heard such horror stories.

"Would you prefer if we talked with someone else present? I understand how it might not seem appropriate for you to be alone with an outsider so soon after..." Your husband's death, John was going to say, but decided that would be callous and just allowed his sentence to drift and for her to come to her own conclusion.

"I think that would be better, Mr. Fisher. My sister is visiting me early evening. Would it be possible for you to return at seven?"

"Of course, Mrs. Miller. I understand how difficult this must be for you."

Emma nodded and smiled.

John couldn't help but smile back. He turned and was about to step off the porch to return to his car, but he stopped and took a minute to take in the view. "This place just doesn't change, does it?" he said, not really directing the question at Emma.

"You've been here before?"

"Oh yes, Mrs. Miller, I've been here before," John said, turning to face the pretty young widow again. "I used to live here."

He left then, before she could ask any more questions, because being back already overwhelmed him too much without having to reminisce with a stranger about the life he had been torn from.

As usual, Ruth arrived too late for Emma to have the time to fill her in on the details of the lawyer's visit before the sound of the approaching luxury vehicle could be heard.

Emma had managed to mumble about finding herself in a bit of a spot, financially speaking, but there was certainly no time for further specifics. Ruth kept repeating all she had already told her. That the lawyer had said that the matter was nothing to worry about, so she really should try to calm down.

The sisters opened the door together and once again John found himself a little taken aback. Now not one, but two pretty young Amish women to deal with. The sister was introduced as Ruth and he noticed that she didn't stop staring at him. Emma ushered him to the dining table and offered him a coffee.

"Coffee sounds excellent," said a beaming John, trying his best to put Emma at ease.

"Cake?" asked Ruth, knowing that Emma wasn't short of comfort food. Every visitor since David's death had arrived with an edible of some sort; Emma had enough to keep her going for the month.

"Why not," agreed John, knowing how regularly coffee and cake used to be served in his home when he was boy.

The two sisters rushed off to the kitchen and John busied himself pulling documents out of his briefcase.

As soon as they were alone in the kitchen, Ruth whispered to Emma excitedly, "You didn't tell me that he was so handsome."

He was handsome, Emma had to agree but speaking about it wasn't really appropriate at this time. It was the sort of ill-judged statement that upset people in the community.

"You know, it wasn't the first thing that leapt to mind!" she replied in sheer exasperation. "When your husband dies and an *Englisch* lawyer in an expensive suit shows up at your door, I can promise you that's the last thought to enter your mind." Emma knew she was a little short with her sister and couldn't decide if it was because she feared the reason behind the lawyer seeking her out, or because she was confused by the strong attraction she felt for him.

Ruth realized her mistake. "Sorry," she said. "I wasn't thinking."

"That's okay," Emma said with a sigh, knowing she needed her sister on her side. She dropped her voice to no more than a hiss. "He is very handsome."

The sisters smiled as they made to serve the coffee and cake.

John took a preemptive bite into the slice of cake and chewed. Suddenly all the old memories came flooding back. The smell of the coffee and the taste of the cake, which he hadn't had occasion to taste since he left the community, triggered the memories from long ago.

He remembered his mother and father being happy before the dreaded cancer became an unwelcome part of their lives. He remembered the love he had felt from his parents and then how it was all so cruelly taken away from him. How different life would have been if his mother hadn't taken ill.

Chances were he wouldn't have left the community. He might even have ended up marrying one of these two girls. There was something about the second sister that brought back some vague memory.

"This cake is really good," complimented John. "I haven't had this in years."

He looked carefully at Emma's sister. "Ruth? Ruth Byler? Don't I remember you from school? Weren't you the girl who used to argue all the time with the teacher?"

The two sisters looked at each other and laughed. "*Jah*. That would be me," agreed Ruth.

John turned to look at Emma who was chuckling softly.

"She still argues any chance she gets," Emma added in a playful tone. John couldn't help but notice that for a woman who had lost her husband only a few days ago, she didn't seem to be grieving as would be expected.

"I can't seem to place you, though, Mr. Fisher," Ruth asked with a flirtatious grin.

John smiled, enjoying the attention of the two beautiful women. He remembered Ruth Byler very well, but he couldn't seem to place her sister Emma at all. Emma look younger than Bruce, and he decided it was probably because they weren't the same age.

"You don't? Seems I didn't make as big an impression on you as you did on me back then," said John, sipping his coffee.

"I wouldn't say that. I wouldn't say that at all," Ruth said in a tone that made it clear she was enjoying John's company. "I see you left the community then?"

John nodded, not wanting to make the conversation personal. "Yes, we left when I was twelve."

"I thought I would have remembered if you'd attended singings," Ruth said with a flirtatious chuckle.

When Emma sighed, John glanced at her and noticed her irritated expression. Could it be because her sister was openly flirting with him, or because the conversation had turned away from the reason for his visit.

"So, Mr. Fisher," began Emma, determined to find out what on earth the lawyer wanted and to stop Ruth's obvious forwardness. "Can you explain why you need to see me?"

John gently rubbed his hands together to get rid of the last crumbs of the cake and reached for a document in front of him.

"Yes, Mrs. Miller. My firm acted in the interests of your late husband David Miller. I have to say that I was not personally handling your husband's affairs. And it also has to be said your husband had not been a client for very long. So you will have to excuse me if I'm a little sketchy on some of the details."

Emma nodded her head as if to say that was all acceptable.

John smiled apologetically in appreciation of Emma's understanding. He reached over and handed her the document he'd been holding. "This is a last will and testament that my firm drew up for your husband less than a fortnight ago. Do you have any idea what it contains?"

Emma looked shocked. Why would David be drawing up a last will and testament just days before he died?

"I have absolutely no idea," Emma said, hurriedly trying to read the document. She moved the paperwork toward Ruth so that she could also read it.

"The document contains a fair amount of legalese. I'm sure you are more than capable of understanding most of it without my help, but if you like, I could give you a short summary to spare you some time?" John offered kindly.

"That would be kind," said Emma, pushing the will away.

"Essentially this will leaves you, as Mr. Miller's widow, a restaurant, which I believe is located here in Holmes County, four properties and a farm in Pennsylvania. It also leaves another farm to Mr. Miller's sister," John moved some of his papers in front of him. "Beatrice Miller?"

Emma was stunned. Unable to comprehend what John was saying. However, could David be leaving farms and properties in his will? They had been scratching for a living and to cover the rent on a restaurant and a house. Why on earth would they be doing that if David owned property and land? It didn't make sense. She sat in silence, contemplating the situation, unable to take it all in.

"Mrs. Miller?" John pressed. "Is that right? Is your husband's sister a Beatrice Miller?"

"Yes," confirmed Emma, coming back to the present. "Although I have to say I've never met her. She lives somewhere in Missouri. For some reason she didn't attend the wedding. To be honest, David didn't speak very much about her. I didn't even know where to contact her to let her know about David's death."

"I see," said John, making a short note about Beatrice Miller. "The properties and land mentioned in the will. Do you have the deed documents that relate to them?"

Emma looked at Ruth perplexed, hoping she could explain. But of course Emma knew she couldn't. "No. I have no deeds. This is the first I've heard about them. My husband didn't mention a thing."

John's heart sank; this was going to make matters difficult. "Right," he said, letting out a frustrated sigh.

"So what does this all mean for my sister?" demanded Ruth, who had immediately grasped the concept that properties and land meant wealth. Her eyes suddenly reminded him of a vulture circling its prey.

"Well, very simply it means that the properties and land David Miller owned in Pennsylvania now belong to your sister. In addition to that, all the income and rents from those properties also belong to your sister. I kind of assumed that there would be a bank account somewhere that holds the rental money?" he looked expectantly at Emma.

She shook her head, "I don't think so. To be honest, Mr. Fisher, my husband and I were struggling with money issues. This house is rented. The restaurant building is also rented, plus there is a loan that needs repaying to the bank that my husband took out to pay for refurbishments. There simply isn't a mystery bank account bursting with money somewhere. David would surely have used it to pay for the refurbishment; he wouldn't have bothered with a loan."

Emma looked at her sister, completely confused. "He wouldn't have burdened us with worry. We wouldn't have had to scratch to find rent money if he had access to wealth. Would he?"

Ruth shrugged her shoulders, as lost as her sister.

John listened to Emma's explanation and became confused. What Emma was saying didn't make sense. Well, actually it made perfect sense. If there was a bank account full of money and properties being rented, then surely that money would have been used to help support the couple.

"I don't understand. Don't you as David's lawyer know about these properties? Where are they? How big are they?" Ruth asked John.

"Unfortunately we don't know. Your sister's husband was due to return to our offices with all the details, but unfortunately he had his accident before that was possible."

"Murder, Mr. Fisher," corrected Ruth. "My brother-in-law was murdered."

"Ruth," hissed Emma. "All of that is in the hands of the police."

John frowned. The partners at his law firm mentioned nothing about a murder. He hadn't looked into how David Miller had died but now he made a mental note to have one of the paralegals find out for him. John glanced at Emma and could see her discomfort at her sister bringing up the subject before turning to Ruth.

"Come on, Emma, Mr. Fisher must know what happened. It's no secret. As a lawyer I'm sure he can come to his own conclusions," insisted Ruth.

Emma was in no mood to argue with her sister, especially in front of the handsome *Englischer* lawyer. She was sure that he kept staring at her a little longer than was necessary, but she couldn't be sure.

"So what happens now?" Emma asked, as she turned back to John. None of what he had just said made sense. She wouldn't outright tell him he was lying, but surely she would have known if David was a wealthy man. She was certain this was all just a misunderstanding or a mistake, perhaps even another David Miller that had left his will and testament, whose wife was also by coincidence named Emma Miller. At this moment that made more sense than imagining her financially troubled husband was indeed a wealthy man.

That's a very good question, thought John suddenly realizing that there might be more to this job than it first appeared. "Well, we need to identify the properties in question somehow, and establish proof of ownership. Do you know of a place where your husband would have kept paperwork? A study, an office?"

Emma looked around and almost burst out laughing "A study? Mr. Fisher the house is barely big enough for this table. We certainly don't have a study."

"But there must be paperwork somewhere, Emma?" Ruth insisted. "Can you think where?"

Emma just stared back blankly and shook her head.

"Well, we will have to search for it," Ruth said, standing up.

"Now?" questioned Emma glancing nervously around the small house. It wasn't that she minded searching; she just didn't want to do it with a stranger present.

"There is no need to look right at this minute, ladies," said John, waving Ruth back into her chair. "But without the paperwork, we simply can't proceed with any certainty. I have checked in at the motel just outside of town. My suggestion is that you have a search around the house, anywhere you think paperwork might be. Chests of drawers, on top of wardrobes. Anywhere. I will talk to my partners in the office and I will come back tomorrow to discuss where we are at."

"How about noon?" suggested Emma immediately. "You could stay for a meal." She knew she sounded a little overeager, but the prospect of David hiding a certain amount of wealth had her on edge, and the sooner she got to the bottom of this the better. She wouldn't admit to secretly looking forward to seeing the handsome *Englischer* again.

"But I'll be at work," said Ruth, looking slightly stunned. Emma had always been one to follow convention, and it wasn't like her to invite a stranger into her home without having a chaperone present.

"I know, but I'm sure Mr. Fisher has many other matters that he needs to be getting on with. I don't want to delay him here for no reason. I'll be fine, Ruth. Mr. Fisher is obviously very respectable, and he understands our community. There is nothing to worry about."

"That's fine. Lunch it is then." John hurriedly packed his case and stood. "Thank you for the coffee and cake. I'm sorry that we haven't got answers for you, Mrs. Miller, but I'm sure they won't be far behind. I'll see myself out, no need for you to walk with me." He nodded a warm smile at both Ruth and Emma and strode confidently for the door.

The two sisters followed his every step with their eyes.

As soon as the door closed behind David, Ruth turned to Emma with a cocked brow. "David was rich?"

Emma laughed wryly. "I was his wife, Ruth. I think if David was rich, I would've known. We're barely scraping by as it is. I'm sure there's some kind of mistake."

Ruth sighed impatiently. "I know, *Mamm* mentioned a few times how tight things were for you. But why would David leave the will listing a number of properties if he didn't own them? I'm not going to stay for dinner after all, but I think you'd better think on that."

Before Emma could argue or insist that Ruth stay for dinner, her sister stood up and left, leaving her alone with her troubled thoughts.

Chapter Four

~

An unwelcome visit

Emma had endured a difficult night. After John Fisher had left for his motel room, Emma bared her soul to her sister. She told her all about her financial difficulties and how she'd only married David because it was what their mother wanted.

Ruth was still subdued, feeling snubbed that Emma would arrange another meeting with the handsome *Englisch* lawyer without her being present, and she wasn't particularly helpful. She could not see past the will. More than once she told her sister, "Emma, you are rich now. It should be me coming to you for help."

She simply couldn't understand that if they couldn't find the documents that related to the properties in the will, Emma was going to stay poor for a very long time. It was highly unlikely that the landlords of either the house or the restaurant would wait until the matter was resolved to receive their money. The *Englisch* bank certainly wouldn't wait!

After Ruth had left for her own home, still not understanding how Emma could be so despondent, Emma spent the best part of the night tearing her own small house to pieces in search of the elusive paperwork. She had no joy. More than once, she sat down with coffee and prayed, asking God for help and guidance. But God did not seem to wish to answer that night. Even when she finally crawled to bed, sleep did not come to relieve her poor tortured mind. She tossed and turned for what seemed like an eternity, trying to think where the mysterious papers might be hidden. And all the time, the handsome face of John Fisher kept dancing into her mind.

She was up early, she couldn't sleep, so why not? She immediately began thinking about the noon meal and started pulling out drawers for the second time, seeing if she missed something the night before. She hadn't. She made a decision about the meal, though: chicken and mountains of mashed potato, together with fresh vegetables picked from the garden that hadn't seen a lot of attention for the last two weeks.

It seemed like a healthy meal for a strapping *Englisch* lawyer and she busied herself in the kitchen, trying to put her worries behind her. She began to bake bread. No Amish meal was complete without bread. She always thought that homes smelt more welcoming with the aroma of freshly baked bread, and she wanted John Fisher to feel welcome in her house. At a little past ten, a knock came to her door.

The lawyer wasn't due for another two hours yet. Emma guessed that it was probably someone else in the community coming to do their good deed for the day and check up on her. She looked into the corner of the kitchen where the gifts of food had been placed and decided that she couldn't accept any more cake or cookies, otherwise she would be the size of a house herself.

Emma opened the door to find Eli King, her landlord, with his straw hat in hand as though trying to use it as protection, like a medieval shield.

"Eli, *gut* morning," said Emma, wiping her flour covered hands on a red towel. What does he want, Emma thought?

"*Gut* morning, Emma. I'm sorry I haven't visited before now. But I thought that there would be many others visiting, I didn't want to intrude. I wanted to see how you were bearing up."

"It's very kind of you to take the time to visit now, Eli," said Emma with a suspicious smile. "I am doing as well as expected. Under the circumstances."

Eli King nodded. "Yes, under the circumstances. That's *gut*," he said, looking at the ground with what could only be described as embarrassment. He obviously had something else he wanted to add.

"Is there something else, Eli?"

Eli looked up and went red. "*Jah*. I'm rather afraid there is."

Emma felt her spirits drop at the thunderous expression on Eli's face. Everyone in the community knew Eli King, and although he was a rumored bully no one had the courage to stand up to him. Least of all Emma.

She stood back and opened the door wider to allow Eli in. Even if she didn't want to hear what he had to say, in essence she was living on his property, so she had no choice but to hear him out.

Eli stepped past her and as soon as he was through the door his eyes darted around the house as if searching for any sign of deterioration or vandalism. Emma had only lived in the house for three months and had done her best to keep it clean and neat.

Without asking, Eli headed to the kitchen where he leaned a hip against the counter and crossed his arms over his chest. He was somewhere in his late fifties or early sixties, his bushy gray brows guarding mean black eyes as they zoned in on Emma.

Emma tried to summon a smile and to convince herself there was nothing to be afraid of. "Would you like *kaffe*?"

Eli shook his head, clenching his jaw. He didn't move and pegged Emma with a malicious look.

Emma felt the hair rise on the back of her neck beneath his scrutinous gaze. The seconds ticked by as if they were hours while Emma waited for him to tell her the reason for his visit. When he finally opened his mouth, Emma exhaled.

"As you are aware, the lease agreement was between me and Mr. Miller?" Eli began.

"Yes, I'm aware."

"That means, Mrs. Miller, that you are not my tenant." Eli waited a few seconds for the words to sink in before he continued. "And as such you have no right to live here. I'm sure you can understand that as a businessman myself I need to look after my own interests. I've heard rumors that you and David were struggling financially these last few months, and I'm sure you'll understand that I can't have a property with dead rent."

"But Mr. King, we paid our rent," Emma said fervently.

"Yes, my dear, you did. But how long can you afford to pay the rent without David here to help you?"

Emma felt her knees buckle beneath her and she moved to the table to sit down. She should have expected this to happen when she opened the door to Eli King, but the reality of what he was saying was even more devastating than only the thought of it.

She glanced down at her clasped hands on the table as she listened to Eli using pretty words to basically tell her that she had to leave as soon as possible. She was no longer welcome on his property and he already had a new family eager to move in.

Even as Eli spoke Emma couldn't help but question why God was doing this to her? It was as if in three short months the entire wall that been torn apart and turned upside down was now being washed down the drain. She knew that God spoke of giving strength to those in need, but right now she felt no strength. She felt like a dishrag that had been used to scrub for hours before being wrung out and now left to dry on the line.

She was only twenty-two years old, and already tired of fighting. Her mother's estate wasn't yet finalized, and now while having to deal with her husband's estate too, she was notified that she was being evicted from her home. The punches didn't stop coming, and Emma didn't know how many more she would be able to take.

For a moment she considered walking out of the kitchen and ignoring Eli, to find a spot where she could cry until there was nothing left to cry about. How she wished right now her mother was here, not to ask for advice, but so that she could see the mess this arranged marriage had left her in.

Chapter Five

The search

The motel thankfully had Wi-Fi, and when he returned to his room John was greeted by a stream of emails that Carol had sent him at the end of the day. At two minutes to midnight he finally managed to get through the last one. He opened a beer from a six pack he had purchased on the way back from the Miller house and sat on the floor, trying to concentrate on some awful television program.

He failed.

He kept seeing Emma Miller's sad and scared eyes in his mind. Brown eyes. Warm and mysterious but filled with so much fear and pain. He could also see her sister Ruth's hungry eyes. Brilliant blue eyes that followed him wherever he went and sang of mischief.

Both women were pretty, and being Amish they wore no makeup, so theirs was a natural beauty. In a different time, a different world, he could see himself being interested in both of them for different reasons. But he wasn't in their world anymore. He was no longer an eight-year-old Amish boy. He was an *Englisch* lawyer and he had to be professional. But Emma Miller's eyes, those wonderful, mysterious eyes, came to him in his dreams. He wondered what they would look like without the fear and pain, and he knew he had to make sure he helped her.

He telephoned Karl Seymour in the office at 6:30 a.m. sharp. Unsurprisingly for a hard working trial lawyer, Seymour answered, already having downed two cups of ink black coffee. John explained the situation and Seymour told him to stay put and get the matter sorted as soon as possible. He reinforced the fact that he needed him back in the office to help prepare for the trial. He then followed up with a short rant about the expense and wasted time and laid the blame fully at Malcolm Kennedy's door. John said that he would do his very best to resolve the situation quickly, the last thing he wanted to do was stay in Holmes County any longer than was necessary.

When he arrived at Emma Miller's house a few minutes before noon, he found the young widow in a flood of tears. She opened the door in a fit of apologies.

"I'm so sorry. The food isn't quite ready yet. I'm afraid I've had quite a morning of upset," Emma said, highly embarrassed.

John immediately took a clean handkerchief from his pocket and handed it to Emma. "Don't worry, Mrs. Miller, whatever is the matter?" Then he realized that was a stupid question to ask a young woman so recently widowed. Wasn't it obvious what the matter was?

Emma rushed John inside and indicated that he should sit in the same place as he had the previous evening. "I had a visit this morning. From my landlord. He said that…" Emma took a deep breath and tried to fight back the tears. "He said that the lease was in David's name only. And because of that, I had no right to stay in the house. Apparently he's got a young family moving in from Pennsylvania. They both work. The landlord said that basically they were better prospects for paying the rent than I now am."

"I see," John said nodding while removing a yellow legal pad and pen from his case. Lawyers are trained to take notes in any situation. "And how soon did he tell you that you had to move out?"

"As soon as possible, he wants me gone."

"Do you have the lease?" John asked hopefully.

Emma shook her head. "No, I've never seen it."

"Okay. Don't worry, give me the landlord's name and his address and I will make sure to see him on your behalf. Technically speaking, he is probably correct. However, I'm sure I can negotiate some time for you. A month or so in order for you to get something else sorted out. Perhaps you could move in with your sister?"

Emma's tears dried up as she tried to pull herself together. "I can't pay you to do this, Mr. Fisher. I simply don't have the funds."

John smiled his warm smile and flashed his brilliant white teeth, "Don't worry about payment, Mrs. Miller. It will take but a minute and I'm here anyway, aren't I?"

"*Denke*, Mr. Fisher, *denke*. You are so kind."

John held up his hand, brushing off the compliment. "Please, think nothing of it. Will you call me John, if you feel comfortable to do so? Mr. Fisher seems so very formal. I'm surrounded by formality every day of my life; it's nice to feel a little more relaxed around clients. Normally they are boring middle aged men in gray suits."

What they certainly aren't are attractive young Amish widows, thought John, laughing to himself.

He was rewarded by a warm smile from Emma. "*Denke*, John, and you must call me Emma." She shook her head. "I'm far too young to be called Mrs. Miller. As you know we rarely use formal address in the community anyway."

"Emma it is," agreed John. "Look, try not to worry too much about the landlord. While he is probably perfectly within his rights, how is it going to look to the rest of the community to be seen throwing a young widow out onto the streets when she has nowhere else to go? I'm sure something can be sorted out for you."

"But that is part of the problem. Eli King doesn't really care what the rest of the community thinks about him. He is practically a law unto himself. I know the bishop has tried to persuade him in the past to curb his behavior." She laughed. "There was even talk of a shunning. But it's all talk and nothing ever seems to do any good."

"Eli King?" repeated John, biting his lip thoughtfully. "That name is quite familiar to me. I have a fancy that he had a run-in with my father many years ago.

Something about a lease on a barn, if I recall correctly. See! I was remembering details on property even then. I must have been destined for the bar."

"Maybe your father could remember more about it?" Emma asked hopefully, thinking it would be very good to get the lawyer as much information as possible about the character of the man who was Eli King.

John shook his head and pointed his eyes at the floor for a moment. "I'm afraid not, Emma. My father died during the first year I was in law school." He looked up and made a joke of the situation. "He won't be able to help very much, I'm afraid."

Emma went bright red with embarrassment. "I'm so sorry, John. I just didn't realize. Please don't be offended."

"Of course not," replied John, wondering about the kind of world she must have grown up to be so concerned about every single little slip of the tongue.

"How on earth were you meant to know?" John thought that she looked pretty cute when she was embarrassed. He mischievously thought he should try to embarrass her a little more often. "One thing is for certain, I'll pay a little visit to Eli King. If my father couldn't get the better of him then maybe I can. It won't do any harm looking like you have a big city lawyer fighting in your corner anyway, will it?"

"No. I guess it won't," agreed Emma. "Right, let me go and fix the food. It won't be long."

"Emma? The papers. Did you find the deed documents?" asked John, suddenly remembering the real reason for his visit.

Emma shook her head. "*Nee.* Sorry. I should have told you straight away."

This might well be the way out of her problems, she thought, but she couldn't do a thing to help herself. "I've turned the house upside down. Twice. If they were here, I would have found them."

John felt a pang of disappointment. Not finding the deeds was going to make this situation very complicated. Maybe David Miller's sister would have some answers? If only he could get addresses for these elusive properties, he would have something to work with at least. He decided to try to find out what Emma knew about the sister while they ate. Other ideas to resolve the situation flooded his mind.

Trying to trace bank accounts was another option. If he could find the bank account into which the monthly rental was being deposited, that would help. But there again, that would be a long and difficult process. Finding the documents was the quickest and cleanest way to solve the problem. If David Miller was due to return to the firm within a week with the documents in hand, then they must have been stored somewhere local.

A safety-deposit box perhaps? Then an idea hit him. "The restaurant, Emma? Did David keep an office there?"

Realization dawned on Emma's face. "The restaurant! Of course." She had meant to return to it today. But John's unannounced arrival had erased any thought of it from her mind. "Yes, he had a small office there. I used to call it a broom cupboard, because that is what I think it was designed for. Only big enough for a small desk. But there is a filing cabinet in there. He kept all of the restaurant papers locked up in there."

John smiled, at last a breakthrough! "Well that would seem to be the obvious place. My suggestion is that we eat first. Then we will go and search the filing cabinet. The smell of that bread has had my mouth watering since I walked through the door!"

"Sounds good," agreed Emma, and she rushed out to the kitchen to fix things up, feeling a little stupid for not thinking of David's restaurant office herself.

John Fisher was a man who was used to a plastic sandwich delivered in a brown bag from the local deli and a diet Coke for lunch. Once a month he might nip out for a stroll and pick himself up a bowl of chili or a footlong. Not what you might call sophisticated dining. This, however, felt like a meal fit for a king. Fried chicken, moist and tender. Mountains of mashed potato. Mint and carrots fresh from the garden and huge chunks of thick buttered bread. John hadn't enjoyed a meal so much in years.

When Emma chuckled softly, John looked up from his plate was a foolish grin. "What's so funny?"

Emma shook her head, but a smile played on her mouth. "I've never seen a man eat like that. Don't they provide guests with food at the motel?"

It was the first time since their meeting that she didn't look distraught, stressed or present with shadows in her eyes. For a moment John's breath simply caught at her natural beauty.

"They do indeed serve meals at the motel, but not like this. To be honest, I can't remember the last time I ate so well. You have a talent, Emma." John wiped his mouth with a napkin before smiling at her. He watched as her cheeks colored slightly pink and she quickly averted her gaze.

"It's just a meal, nothing special."

John shook his head before reaching for the tall glass of water. He took a sip, watching over the rim of the glass. "It's not just a meal. People don't cook like this in the city. Especially not bachelors like me who live alone. Most nights we fall back on takeaways or microwave meals."

Emma's brows drew together in confusion. "Microwave meals? Do you mean those little box things you get in the freezer section at the supermarket?"

John chuckled. "Now that you mention it, I'm sure it's not very nutritious." He tilted his head slightly and searched her face. "David was a very lucky man to have a woman like you cooking for him every night."

The mention of her deceased husband's name darkened Emma's eyes before she quickly looked away. "Would you like some more?"

John realized she was diverting the conversation and decided to let it go. He glanced down at his empty plate and knew he couldn't really stomach another bite, but he nodded yes anyway. "If you can spare some, I'd love a little more mashed potatoes and vegetables."

Emma laughed softly as she stood up and reached for his plate. "An Amish man would've asked for more meat."

This time it was John who felt shadows of his past

come back to haunt him. "Good thing I'm not Amish anymore then, isn't it?"

She served another plate and returned to the table. This time John decided to direct the conversation toward the purpose for his visit. "Tell me about Beatrice Miller?"

While they ate, John got some background on the sister in Missouri, Beatrice Miller. Emma couldn't tell him all that much since she had never met the woman. David had not mentioned her all that much. From what Emma had gathered, she had never even been baptized into the community.

There had been a big falling out regarding just that within the family many years ago. A falling out so drastic that David had himself fallen out with his own parents. Apparently he had tried to keep the peace but ended up fighting with both the sister and the parents. He had moved up to Pennsylvania for a year or so afterward, before finally ending up in Holmes County where he had been for the last five or six years. But no one hereabouts knew anything in detail about his background. When Emma had asked David about inviting Beatrice to the wedding, he had told her that she'd already been invited but had refused to attend.

However, in hindsight, she wasn't completely sure that had been the truth. Certainly, she couldn't find contact details for the mysterious sister when it came to letting her know that her brother had died. John nodded his head wisely as Emma related the tale. He could relate completely. When his father left the Amish community, his brother stopped speaking to him completely.

A proper shunning. Unfortunately his uncle followed his father to the grave within months, without the two men ever having made up. John knew that Beatrice Miller had to be found.

So he made a mental note to email Carol, advising her to get a paralegal to work on a search. For all they knew Beatrice Miller could be dead too. She could be married. Anything. This case was getting more complex by the minute.

John tried to help Emma clear up, but she wouldn't hear a word of it. She settled him in an old rocking chair and said she would be no longer than twenty minutes. John didn't argue. He sneakily checked his iPhone. No signal. Amazing, he thought. People actually live like this. No interruptions, no hassle and the majority of the time, no stress.

For the first time this morning John had actually hit snooze on his phone when it rudely awoke him from his slumber. It was the first time that had happened since he started work. Okay, he was still on the phone to his managing partner at 6:30. But he wasn't in the shower at 4:30. Sleep was good. He looked out the window and watched three Amish men move some modern ploughing equipment by hand. Hard physical work. He'd forgotten what that was like.

He did a bit when he was in law school, trying to put food on his table. He'd enjoyed it. Hard work. Good for the soul. He wondered if the Amish men pushing the plough knew what life was like outside their community. He decided that they couldn't possibly know. They might think they knew what life was like, but you had to experience it for yourself.

John had hardly ever considered what life might be like back here in Holmes County. The pain of losing his mother and then being uprooted from the only home he had ever known was too much. He realized that he somehow blamed the Amish way of life for his mother's death. Irrational, he knew. Maybe now that he understood it, he could stop the blame. Blame only caused more pain.

Emma came back smiling and carrying two massive mugs of coffee. "We'll drink these first, then go and find those missing documents."

John re-entered the present. And as he sipped his coffee, he realized that after just one meal and twenty minutes in a rocker, he had managed to identify his chief demon. What might happen if he stayed longer, he wondered as he looked at Emma drinking her coffee. It was an intriguing thought.

Chapter Six

The restaurant

Emma had rarely been in a car. Certainly she had never been in such an expensive one. The range of flashing lights, electronic readouts and controls was mind blowing to her.

"Are you warm enough?" asked John, reaching down and pressing a button. "There, I've turned the seat heat up for you."

"Seat heat?" laughed Emma in delight. "We don't get that in a buggy!"

John laughed too, and Emma felt her tummy flip with excitement.

Then she felt shame. Her husband had recently died, how could she be enjoying another man's company quite so much? She knew the answer straight away, although she wasn't proud of it, and she knew that tonight she would pray for *Gott*'s guidance on. She knew that she may have been married on paper. But in her heart, where it truly mattered, she knew she had never felt love for David. She was upset by his death, sorry about his death even, and she was certainly overwhelmed by all of it. But did she really feel grief at his passing? She didn't know.

It took about ten minutes to get to the restaurant. The car park looked pretty empty.

Stephanie, the other server, flung open the door and hugged her. "Oh Emma, I'm so sorry. Poor David. I mean…"

Stephanie was a young *Englisch* girl whom David had employed a little while after taking Emma on. The two had become friends, but this was the first time she had seen Emma since the news of David's death broke. She was at a loss for words.

"*Denke*, Stephanie," said Emma. "And *denke* from the bottom of my heart for the hours you've put in here since…" Emma dried up, for some reason not wanting to say the words. "Well you know, since David's death."

The two women broke the embrace. "No worries, Emma. I wish I could tell you I'd been rushed off my feet. But I can't say I have. We've had a couple of busy days, but most have been slow. At least it stops Jason complaining."

Emma laughed at Stephanie's joke about her brother Jason. The chef wasn't a man that liked working in a high pressure environment. She may have been laughing but inside she felt a bolt of fear. She could really have done with Stephanie saying that takings were up, and the business was making more money than ever before. Emma was disappointed, but not surprised.

"This is John Fisher, Stephanie," Emma introduced, standing aside and indicating John. "He is a lawyer. He's come to help me with David's will."

Stephanie reached out and shook John's hand, giving Emma a slight raise of the eyebrows in the process. A secret indication that she thought John was a very attractive man.

Emma turned to John, deciding she wanted to get him out of Stephanie's sight. She'd seen Stephanie hand *Englisch* customers her cell phone number with their bill before now. David never knew, of course. If he did, Stephanie would have been looking for a new job. But Emma thought it rather funny, something that she could see her sister Ruth doing if she had a cell phone!

They all went inside, and Jason came out of the kitchen to offer his condolences on her loss. Emma accepted them with thanks.

John wasn't sure what he expected from a restaurant that was owned and managed by an Amish couple, but he wasn't expecting this. The restaurant seemed like any restaurant back in the city.

The walls were painted a dark hue of olive green. It might not have been this tasteful in any other setting, but the black and white photos in thick white frames that lined the walls gave it a classy atmosphere. The tables were all oak, with comfortable chairs to encourage the patrons to relax. A small vase of flowers stood on every table, along with a banner displaying the day's specials. There was a coffee bar in the corner that boasted the latest in restaurant-grade coffee machines and a variety of beans. The scent of coffee hung in the air, welcoming him and making him want to spend a little time there.

He couldn't help but be impressed by the caliber of the restaurant David Miller had left to his wife. The only problem was there wasn't a single patron in sight.

"The restaurant is very nice," John said to Emma.

Emma smiled but the shadows remained in her eyes. "It is, I just wished it would be busier." She glanced at Stephanie and Jason before turning back to John. "Shall we go to the office?"

John nodded, for a moment he had completely forgotten the purpose of his visit to the restaurant. "Yes, the sooner we get those papers, the sooner I can get back to Cleveland."

Being in Holmes County was throwing him off kilter. John had always been organized, to the point, and focused on the task at hand. But ever since arriving in Holmes County and meeting the beautiful widow Miller, he found himself more and more distracted by the life he had left behind fifteen years ago.

"You were right," laughed John when Emma opened the door. "It's not very big, is it?"

"I wasn't lying," replied Emma as they walked in. There was barely enough room for both of them and Emma took a silent gasp of breath as John brushed past her on his way to the filing cabinet. Her stomach flipped and once again she felt guilty for being attracted to her husband's lawyer. It didn't occur to her that her marriage wasn't one of love; it only occurred to her that regardless of the circumstances surrounding the marriage, she should be loyal to the memory of her deceased husband.

"Locked," said John, pulling on the top drawer. "Do you have a key?"

"It's up there on that high shelf, under that small stack of menus," Emma said, pointing at a pile of printed table menus.

John moved past her again and once again her stomach started dancing. She had never experienced anything like this before. Emma had never felt her nerve endings light up in the presence of a man. It was a strange feeling, but one that she oddly enjoyed. She pushed the thought aside and decided to instead focus on the purpose of being in the office instead of how John's presence was assaulting her senses, albeit pleasantly.

Emma would have had to have stood on tip toe to reach up to get the key, but John was so tall he reached it with ease. He moved back to the cabinets, turned the key and pulled open the first drawer. It was safe to say that David was not a man who liked to keep things organized. There were papers hung up in files, and papers stacked in bundles, without any obvious system to any of it. John pulled open each of the five drawers in turn to reveal a similar scenario.

"Ah yes," Emma said, peering into the bottom drawer. "I kept telling David he needed a better system for filing everything. He never listened, of course."

John returned to the top drawer, pulled out a stack of documents and placed then on the surprisingly tidy desk. "There is nothing for it; we are just going to have to go through everything piece by piece."

John knew what he was looking for, so he was far quicker than Emma, who hadn't been trained to read through a document at lightning speed. By the time they had reached halfway through the fourth drawer, John began to fear that the documents weren't there. He also knew that the restaurant that had been granted to Emma in the will was not much of a business at all. Records upon records of late payments, demands for money and numerous other concerns. Unless he could get his hands on these property documents quickly, he didn't know what on Earth she was going to do.

By the time they pulled the last stack of documents from the bottom drawer, John knew that the property documents weren't going to be there. But there was one small breakthrough.

A piece of paper, torn from a reporter's notebook, fell to the floor. Emma bent to pick it up, reading what it said.

"Look," she said excitedly. It simply read "Beatrice" and gave a cell phone number. For the last thirty minutes she had been reminded of how dire the situation was, and finding Beatrice's number could hopefully answer some of the questions she had.

"Well, at least it's something," said John, trying to remain positive. "But the deeds are not here."

Emma nodded despondently. If David had any important documents, she had been sure they would've been here. Thirty minutes of searching had only yielded

Beatrice's phone number and John had been privy to the number of late-payment notices she had been trying to forget ever since the funeral.

She couldn't help but feel ashamed of the debt she was in. For some reason it mattered to her that John didn't think of her as irresponsible, but then she hadn't brought on this debt.

"Hopefully Beatrice can help," Emma said hopefully.

"What I'm going to do is speak to my office. We have paralegals who know how to break bad news to people. We have to do it all the time. I'm afraid someone in your family has died, but we come bearing gifts. That sort of thing. Hopefully the paralegal can make contact with Beatrice and then we can go from there," said John, immediately outlining his strategy.

Emma nodded her agreement. "I'll get us a coffee while you make the call," she said, disappearing out the door.

Stephanie immediately came over to join her at the coffee machine. There were just two men in the restaurant, each tucking into a burger special. "Your lawyer is pretty good-looking. Where did you find him from?"

"I didn't," insisted Emma. "David did."

She hoped that Stephanie didn't notice the blush that was now coloring her cheeks.

"Single?" Stephanie asked with a wink.

Emma grinned before leaving Stephanie and taking the two cups of coffee back to the office. "I haven't asked!"

John smiled as she reentered the office with the drinks. "Lovely," he said, taking a little sip of the hot drink. "A paralegal is going to telephone. Let's see what happens."

"So what do we do about these deed documents now?" asked Emma.

"I'm convinced they must be stored locally. And this is our next lead." He held up an invoice he had plucked from the piles of paperwork in the filing cabinet. It was for a self-storage unit a few miles away. "This invoice seems to suggest a unit there that has been paid up for the next ten months. Any ideas what is in it?"

Emma shook her head. "Something else I know nothing about," she said with a sigh.

Next time she found herself in an arranged marriage, Emma made a mental note to find out more about the man she was marrying. At least then she wouldn't feel like a *ferhoodled* nitwit if something happened. A frown creased her brow as she met John's questioning gaze. "Although, come to think of it, I know the storage place itself. My mother never owned a barn or any outbuildings in which to store stuff. She had a unit there for years. I don't really know what she kept there. Rubbish mainly, I guess, given that she never actually threw anything out. I don't know why she went to the expense, to be honest."

There seems to be a good deal you don't know about your husband, thought John to himself. "Well I guess we have to look there next. Would you like to come with?"

Emma knew that it would probably be expected of her to see what her husband had hidden in the storage room, but she couldn't summon the energy. After dealing with his funeral and realizing the amount of debt she was in, she had barely spent any time at the restaurant. She appreciated that Stephanie and Jason had taken the reins but knew that, as the new owner, she had to get involved sooner or later.

The restaurant was her only lifeline at this stage if she wanted to crawl her way out of the mountain of debt. "To be honest, John, I should probably spend a few hours here. I feel bad that I have left everything to Stephanie and Jason. Would you mind awfully if you went on your own?"

"No, not at all," replied John, feeling a little upset that he wouldn't get to spend any more time with the attractive widow. He had quite enjoyed her company, and there was something about her that intrigued him. Something peaceful and calming. Like walking into a church and immediately being washed over with serenity.

For such a long time John had been immersed in ambition and greed, that he had forgotten what it was like to spend time with people who valued faith, family, and community above everything else.

"I will go and have a look. You'll need to write me a short letter of authorization, just to be on the safe side. I want to try to see our friend Mr. King as well. But I think that had better wait till the morning, I think this is more important." He picked up a stack of table menus and glanced over the varied selection, surprised at the low prices compared with the city standards. "Your breakfast looks good. Shall I meet you here for breakfast, say nine thirty? My treat."

"You don't need to pay," began Emma, waving her hands in the air in protest.

"Emma, I've seen what's in those filing cabinets. Final demands and the like. Besides, these prices aren't even half of what I would've paid for a similar meal in the city!" he said with a grin. "But don't worry, I feel we are getting close now. As soon as we have the documents, you are going to be okay. I'm sure of it. Now, will you be all right getting home?"

Emma nodded, appreciating his kindness. "Yes, I'll stay till Stephanie and Jason finish. I'm sure they won't mind giving me a lift home, it's not far off their path."

John's cell phone let out an electronic alert, and he looked at the screen. He frowned and gave a slight shake of the head. "That was a message from the paralegal. Beatrice isn't answering the phone. But she left a message. Hopefully at some point today she will ring back."

"More waiting then," said Emma, with a raise of her eyebrows.

"Not for me," said John, slipping his jacket back on. "I'm off to see what is in this storage unit. You need to write me that authorization."

Emma nodded, reaching for a pad of paper. Maybe it was better if she didn't go with John. Apart from the debt she had discovered since David's death, she was afraid of the skeletons yet to be revealed that might well be jumping out of the closet. For all she knew, the debt was the least of her worries.

Chapter Seven

The sister

Driving to the storage yard, John got a call from Karl Seymour on his mobile phone. Seymour was stressed. There had been some coverage in the press about the trial and plenty of new evidence had shown up out of the blue because of it. Now it really wasn't looking good for Seymour's drug-running, hit man-hiring, teacher friend. Karl wanted John back in the office—the ship was sinking before it had even set sail and it was all hands to the pumps. John expected to feel excitement. But strangely, he didn't. He felt regret.

Ever since attending law school, John had been so focused on his career and making a name for himself that he hadn't taken any time off, unless he was sick. For the first time in years he wasn't in the cutthroat environment where boundaries were constantly pushed, and expectations rose all the time.

It was his first time in a new, if slightly familiar, environment. He'd found it incredibly refreshing. Watching those Amish men pull the plough over lunchtime, each striving for a common cause. Unified. In law it was always a battle. One side won and one side lost. As long as the plough moved and turned the earth, all of those men won during that lunchtime. What a thought.

Everyone winning.

The change of pace and change of scenery had John looking at his life from an entirely new perspective. Holmes County was so different to Cleveland; there wasn't the constant rat race and everyone rushing toward the next victory or big payoff. Life was slower here, and apart from the slower pace, it was good to be surrounded by people who put faith, family and community first. John had never let go of his faith, but he had to admit it had been on the back burner for quite a long time.

In the city you didn't know that someone was religious unless they proved to be Bible-waving lunatics. Here, no one mentioned their religion, but you could see it in their way of life. The way they treated others, and the way the community drew together when they lost one of their own.

Had this been any other place, John would've been eager to get back to Cleveland and get on with the case the partners at tasked him to help with. But this wasn't any other place; this was the home he had left behind so many years ago.

John decided that he wasn't ready to head back to corporateville just yet. He wanted to help Emma Miller. He wanted to see everything made right. He felt rather like a knight in shining armor from the days of old, rescuing the vulnerable and beautiful damsel in distress.

"John, are you still there?" Seymour barked at the other end of the line, causing John to realize he hadn't yet answered him. He quickly came up with a plan and hurriedly told his managing partner a slight untruth.

"Yes, I'm still here. But there has been a slight complication here in Holmes County." John drew in a deep breath and hoped he would be forgiven for the white lie that would provide him opportunity to help Emma Miller. "Mrs. Miller and David Miller's sister are both very unhappy about the way in which the firm has seemed to have handled matters. They feel the will has been unprofessionally executed and are threatening to sue citing incompetence."

He held his breath as he heard Seymour curse on other side of the line. "This is all I need now." Seymour's voice held an edge of agitation.

"I'll take care of this, Seymour, but it's going to take me a little longer than we initially expected. Neither the widow nor Beatrice Miller know the whereabouts of the deed to any of the properties. This morning I discovered the papers to a storage unit on the other side of town. I am headed there as we speak. If I can find the deeds, I'm sure they'll both be elated and forget about the threats."

"I need you back here, John. This case is hanging on by a thread and I need all hands on deck."

"I understand. The sooner I get these documents the sooner I'll be back. I'm going to find out if there's been any word from Beatrice Miller and then I will be meeting with the widow in the morning to set a course of action if the deeds had not yet been found. If all goes well, I could be back by lunchtime tomorrow afternoon."

"I'm not liking this, but I know we need to deal with it. Deal with it, John, and make it snappy."

John was used to Seymour and his short temper and no longer let it intimidate him. "Worst-case scenario I'll be back in the office first thing day after tomorrow."

He could hear a heavy sigh on the other side of the line. "Fine. You sort this out; you know how I feel about legal recourse being taken against my firm, John. I won't have that little turn-up who messed up this will scar the reputation of this firm."

"I'm doing my best. I know that if the press gets word of this it's going to be a circus. An Amish widow taking action against a legal firm in Cleveland; they'll eat it up. That's not going to be good for any of us in the long run."

"We're not even going to go there, just fix this. I'm counting on you," Seymour snapped. Before John could reply, Seymour ended the call.

John drew in a deep breath as a slow smile formed on his mouth. He had just bought himself another thirty-six to forty-eight hours in Holmes County. He wanted to make the best of it. And the only way he was going to do that, was if he could find the deed that would see to it that Emma Miller was left a very wealthy widow.

At the storage yard, the receptionist had to call the supervisor down from the staff room. He wasn't happy because he had his feet up and was trying as best he could to make short work of a footlong. Looking at the man, John thought he could probably have done with skipping the snack anyway. His time would certainly have been better spent helping any number of his customers with their heavy lifting. The supervisor read the paperwork and listened to John's explanation and then called his manager.

Finally, the supervisor appeared out of the office with a pair of bolt cutters. "I assume you don't have the key?" he growled like a bear disturbed out of hibernation.

"Nope," replied John pleasantly, shaking his head.

"Follow me," the bear said with a growl that challenged him to do otherwise.

They walked, at no great pace, for about 120 yards down a long corridor that appeared to be steeped naturally in darkness, but which lit up as you walked down its length. It reminded John of something he had seen on *The X-Files* when he was a teenager, and he half expected Mulder and Scully to appear at any moment. The bear stopped at 365, a unit no more than six feet wide, and brought the bolt cutters into play. John heard a crack and the padlock fell to the floor.

"You can get a new one for five bucks before you leave," said the bear, and he ambled back down the corridor, leaving John in his pool of light and the blackness of the long corridor beyond.

He lifted up the steel shutter and reached around inside for a light switch. He found the switch and flicked it on. An array of what appeared to be junk stared back at him. His heart sank. He was hoping for a filing cabinet or possibly one of those portable safe units. But there seemed to be nothing within the unit at first glance that might hold important papers. However, John had seen enough of David Miller's method of filing back in the restaurant to suggest that that did not necessarily indicate very much.

Important papers could just as well be stuffed under an old mattress if what he had seen was anything to go by. He poked around, removing dust sheets, hoping to find a box of papers. No such luck. An assortment of broken furniture. A landscape portrait that looked like it had been painted by a student. A strange array of ancient gardening implements. But absolutely nothing of any value or anything that in any way resembled paperwork.

After forty-five minutes of poking about, John conceded defeat and marched back down to the receptionist where he presented a five dollar bill in exchange for a new padlock. He returned to the heartbreak that was unit 365 and snapped the padlock into place. He thought it would have been preferential to leave the unit open and allow any passing chancer to take whatever they wanted. It probably would've been cheaper for Emma in the long run.

He didn't want to mess about in the building. It gave him the spooks, to be honest. As soon as he was out in the car park he pulled out his mobile phone to see if he had received any messages regarding Beatrice Miller. He walked to his car while looking at his smart phone. He was so engrossed in flicking through his messages that he charged directly into a young woman. The poor woman fell to the ground and John bellowed an apology and crouched down beside her to check that he had not caused her any injury. He was surprised to see the face of Ruth Byler staring back at him.

"Why didn't you look where you were…" she angrily demanded, before recognition silenced her. "Oh? Mr. Fisher, it's you."

"Miss Byler. I'm so sorry," said a worried John, going down on one knee and reaching out to steady her as she tried to stand. "I was caught up looking at messages, I'm afraid. Are you okay?"

Ruth got to her feet with John's strong supportive hand for guidance. "No harm done," she said pleasantly, brushing herself down. Although she pretended to be fine, John could see she was a little startled. She rocked back on her heels and John caught her elbow just in time, before she went down again.

"More shock than anything else," Ruth quickly said trying to make light of the situation.

"Look, can I get you a coffee? I'd rather wait with you a few minutes, just to make sure you are okay," asked John.

Ruth gave him a little coy smile. "Here I thought my afternoon was going to be boring, seems I was wrong. I wouldn't say no to having coffee with a handsome man like you, Mr. Fisher."

"Good," said John, flashing the charming smile that women so adored.

"There is a good place just down there," Ruth said, pointing a little way down the road.

"Sounds good," John agreed before he started walking in that direction. A few places later he stopped.

"Hang on? What were you doing here? You were going inside."

"Don't worry," said Ruth. "It was nothing important. I'm just going through some of mother's things to sort out what we'll be keeping and what needs to go. Even though she was a hoarder, there are some big items I think we should keep. She has always kept a storage unit here. I can go inside and look when we've had our coffee."

"I see," said John. "Are you okay walking? You didn't hurt your ankle or anything?" John asked when she swayed again.

Ruth laughed. "I'm fine, Mr. Fisher, just a bit shaken. A coffee will do me the world of good, just to settle my nerves."

They walked down the road and into the coffee house. John ensured that Ruth was seated comfortably, just like a proper gentleman, before going to purchase the drinks.

"*Denke*, Mr. Fisher," said Ruth, as John put down a large steaming mug of coffee in front of her. She smelled the comforting aroma and smiled.

"John. Please call me John," insisted John as he slipped in opposite her in the booth.

Ruth stirred in two large sugars. "Okay, John and I'm Ruth, okay?

"That's better," she said as she sipped her drink. "So what does your girlfriend think about you being away from home, then?"

John smiled at Ruth's clumsy way of asking if he was single. He was used to women approaching him on the few occasions he went out. It never stopped amazing him how bad some of their first lines were. A frown creased his brow at Ruth's forwardness. Although Amish girls were usually reserved, it was clear Ruth didn't inherit that gene.

"No girlfriend, Ruth. I work too much for that."

The words sounded ridiculous even to his own ears, but it was the truth. Even if he carved out enough time to date a little, he wouldn't have time to build any kind of relationship. He couldn't imagine any woman being willing to put up with his schedule. But he was not getting younger. Was work what it was all about? Didn't he want something else as well?

"What were you doing at the storage place, out of interest?" asked Ruth, full of questions.

"It appears that your sister's husband had a unit there himself. I've just been checking it out, to see if these documents were there," replied John.

"They haven't been found, then?" Ruth asked sipping on a coffee. Although the deeds would make Emma a very wealthy woman, John couldn't help but notice the greedy expression in Ruth's gaze.

John paused before he answered. Technically Ruth wasn't a client and he shouldn't share too much information, but he thought there might be an opportunity to lay a little ground work on Emma's behalf.

"No, I'm afraid to say they haven't. Without them we aren't going to get this situation resolved anytime soon. Did you know that Emma's landlord visited her this morning, and basically told her that he wanted her out of the house?"

Ruth sighed. "No! Really?"

John nodded, looking glum.

"That is Eli King all over again. The man has never been very nice," said Ruth, sneering as she spoke the words.

"I suggested that Emma should move in with you for a while. Until the issue of this will is resolved, your sister will be very financially pressed," John said.

"I see," replied Ruth, gazing down at the ground. "I suppose it would be the sensible solution. It would be helpful with the rent that I have to pay. It's just that…" Ruth stopped abruptly as though she would regret what she was about to say.

"It's just what, Ruth?" asked John, his interest raised.

"Well," Ruth replied hesitantly, looking around her to see who might be within earshot. "You promise that this will go no further?"

"Of course," agreed John, raising his hands as if there was no need to ask.

Ruth laughed. "Just like you were my lawyer?"

John laughed back. "That's right, a proper lawyer and client relationship."

Ruth slowly raised her eyes at him. "I'd like that."

John moved his position on the bench and smiled. Was Ruth flirting with him? She couldn't be, surely. "So? What is it?" he asked.

"Emma and me. We've never really got on that well, to be honest. We are both very different people. Emma was always mother's favorite. I knew that from an early age, and I'll be honest, I always resented it. I still do in many ways. Emma is very quiet. She was always the good daughter, the one everyone liked, the one that tried to please everyone and always the one following Mother's wishes. Whereas I was…"

Ruth stopped and considered her words. "Well, I was different. Where Emma could quote Bible phrases, I knew the latest *Englisch* fashions. I just didn't have the interest. Emma is happy staying at home. She never used to take part in the volleyball or other fun things. She did enjoy the singings though, and she has a sweet voice. But I always thought there must be something more to life; I was looking for a bit of excitement. Mother never knew, but there were one or two *Englisch* boys in my teenage years." She raised her eyebrows and smiled at John, who nodded with his own smile, completely understanding. Instead of being ashamed of this fact like most Amish girls would be, Ruth seemed proud of it.

"So, what are you saying, Ruth?" John asked, draining the last of his drink.

"I'm saying that living with Emma would be difficult. I know that and so does she. But, she's my sister and I love her. So, of course I'm not going to see her out on the street or being bullied by the likes of Eli King. So yes, Emma is more than welcome to move in with me anytime she likes. But…" She stopped again and looked around.

"But what?"

"I'm leaving the community, John. I don't want my life to run away without me doing something with it. Ever since *Mamm* passed away, I realized that I only stayed because of her. Because I didn't want to let her down and, for some reason, I believed that sooner or later I would become her favorite. I realize now that I can't hang my happiness on another's door. I need to find it for myself, John. I'm not talking about tomorrow, or even next week or next month, but within the year. I don't want Emma to move in with me, only to have to move out again when I leave."

"I see," said John. "It's a big decision. It's one that I'm glad I didn't have to make myself. It was taken on my behalf by my father."

"You mean when you moved away?"

"Yes. I came home one day to find our belongings in the back of an *Englisch* car waiting to take us away. Coming back here has made me realize how our decision must've been for him."

Ruth nodded in understanding. "It's something I've been toying with for years. I think it was only Mother that was keeping me here. Meeting you yesterday helped me realize that it is something I had to do."

"Meeting me?" questioned John, in a confused tone.

"Absolutely. Look at you; an Amish boy who is now a big-time lawyer. That must be so exciting."

"It has its moments," agreed the outward part of John. The inner part of him said that it was akin to being a prisoner. He had never thought of his career that way but breaking the chains for a few days had made him realize that climbing the corporate ladder had only become a self-imposed jail. Nothing existed outside of his work, no friends or family to break the monotony of chasing the next big deal.

"I'd love to be a lawyer. Or a doctor. Something to make a real difference. I can't do that here," said Ruth sadly. John nodded, although he doubted that Ruth had the tenacity to put in the hard work to become either.

"And I want a husband. Try as I might there is no one in the community I have the remotest interest in or at least not one that lives in the community." She gave John a look that suggested he could well be what she was looking for.

"I truly wish you well, Ruth," replied John, trying to ignore the eyes that bored into his own. It was hard, Ruth was a beautiful woman, and she was so obviously interested in him. It wouldn't take much for him to help find work for her in Cleveland, find her a place and then who knows what? But if he was honest with himself Ruth wasn't the Byler sister that made his heart beat faster. The one that did, had recently lost her husband, and John had never liked settling for second best.

He finished the last of his coffee and met Ruth's gaze. "Just remember Ruth, the grass isn't always greener on the other side. Do remember that before you make a big choice. And please remember your sister; you are the only one she has at the moment. If you were to suddenly uproot and leave, I think she would be quite lost."

"Don't worry, John. I'm not going to abandon her. She is my flesh and blood." She paused for a minute and then said, "But if I come to Cleveland, I'll be sure to look you up."

Chapter Eight

Eli King

Eli King did not look impressed to see an *Englisch* lawyer on his porch.

"How does she afford a lawyer like you?" He sneered after John had introduced himself and said who he was representing.

John smiled and ignored the question. It all came flooding back to him now. He even recognized Eli's face, although obviously now the hair had turned gray and the stomach had grown in size. He remembered that this man had visited their home on a few occasions, probably about six months before his mother died.

He remembered it well, because whenever he visited, his father would always be angry. His mother would try and calm him down and tell him it was the will of God. She insisted that if God did not want his father to have the barn then that was it. John remembered seeing it another way; he remembered seeing this man enter their home and when he left, there would be upset and aggravation. John decided immediately that he wasn't going to allow any more hurt to be caused by this man.

"I understand you have verbally served my client notice to vacate your property, even though she has not yet been a widow for a month," John said, as Eli King was still studying his business card.

"It is regretful, but your client as you call her, was not my tenant. David Miller was. She has no right to stay on my property," replied King, very sure of himself.

"Maybe so but think how it will look within the community; kicking a poor, young, grieving widow into the street," said John, trying to make the man see sense.

King laughed. "I know perfectly well how this community sees me, Mr. Fisher. And secondly I'm hardly kicking the girl out on the street, she only moved from her mother's house a few months ago. She can clearly move back there. And I'm not serving eviction notices either, am I?"

John had to concede that he wasn't. "I understand your position, Mr. King, but the woman has not defaulted on the rent and understandably, at present her emotions are all over the place. I am requesting, politely, that you simply have a heart." He thought for a moment before adding more. "This isn't very Christian, is it?"

"What would you know of it?" Eli King snapped at John, looking him up and down as though he were nothing more than dirt on the floor and would know nothing about being a Christian.

"God's ways are clear to us all," John said, shocking himself in the process. "Listen, Mr. King, my suggestion is this: you give Emma Miller as much time as she needs, and the rent will be paid in full and on time." He'd already decided that if Emma didn't have the rent that month, he would pay. "I will advise my client that at some point, when she feels able, she should start thinking about making alternative arrangements. I don't know long that will take; it may be a few weeks or a few months." John stopped talking, making sure that Eli King was taking it all in.

"She actually likes the house. Who knows, after probate has been resolved on her husband's will she might even choose to buy it off you. Save her from having to move out."

The idea John had was to give the man a little hint that there was money about, but it was a little distance away. If he were to grant Emma a little time, then who knows what might happen. However, Eli King gave John a look that suggested he strongly doubted Emma Miller would be in a position to offer him anything more than a dime for the house.

John hadn't finished yet. "In the meantime you will not hassle my client in any way, shape or form. If you do, Mr. King, I will use all means at my disposal." He smiled warmly as though he were talking to his friend over dinner and not issuing threats. "If you do happen to formalize proceedings, then I can assure you they will be defended, down every avenue. I won't charge Mrs. Miller for my time, so she won't be burdened with bills. I'm guessing the same will not be said for your own legal representation."

"But, but…" stammered Eli King, feeling he had been hit by a sledgehammer.

"Look, Mr. King, let me be perfectly honest and open with you. I just want the pressure off my client for a while, that's all," confirmed John. "She has just been widowed," he said softly but firmly, trying to get over the significance of the point. "God wants us all to be charitable, does he not?" John reached out and patted Eli King's shoulder in a reassuring manner. Eli's only response was to let his mouth hang open. "Now is your time to start with that charity." With that, John turned, went back to his car and drove away, feeling very pleased with himself.

As he drove he called the office. There was still no word from Beatrice, so he asked them to ring again and stress the urgency of the situation. John decided he would visit Emma and fill her in on what had happened since he had left her that afternoon. He looked at his watch and guessed she would be home from the restaurant by now. If not, he would try to catch her there. Emma had the door open before he had even switched off the engine; she had heard the sound of the car approaching and was hoping it was good news.

"Good and bad," replied John when she asked. "The bad is that there was just junk in the storeroom. Pure junk. So we are no closer to finding the deeds."

Emma looked downcast when he told her. "Oh, I was hoping that you were coming with good news. I really could do with some good news; I've just been looking through the restaurant takings since David died. It's not pleasant."

"Well there is good news," said John, smiling as she placed a rather large slice of chocolate cake in front of him. "I went to see our great friend Eli King."

"And?" Emma asked, apprehensively.

John ate the chocolate cake and sipped more of Emma's coffee as he related the story of his encounter with her landlord.

They were both in fits of laughter by the end as John described the look on Eli's face.

"Oh I wish I had been there to see it," giggled Emma.

"I wish you had too," said John, suddenly realizing what a warm and funny person Emma was. It would be great to spend some time with her once all of this was over and she didn't have the worry or grief hanging over her head. "I strongly doubt that you will hear from him in a while. But if you do, then you must contact me. I'll send him a mountain of paperwork and he can bury himself under that." Emma saw John looking at her in a strange way and she hoped that there was something meaningful to the look.

Emma couldn't remember ever feeling this way when a man looked at her. She felt as if she was the only woman in the world, and right now could soar like an eagle if she wanted to. She felt a light blush color her cheeks before she looked away. The reality of the situation came crashing down; John was *Englisch* and she was Amish, and recently widowed she reminded herself.

Needing the conversation to take another direction, she glanced up at John with a furrowed brow. "Do you ever regret that you left the community, John?" asked Emma softly.

"Not till yesterday," said John, looking honestly deep into her sad, lonely eyes.

"Why is that?"

"Because yesterday I realized that the decision to leave had been made for me. Would I have stayed if my father hadn't dragged me away?" John let out a heavy sigh. "That's all bygones now but I have to admit, coming back has been confusing. I have a few demons to work through to understand why."

Emma nodded without saying a word, but John could see the shadows returning to her hazel eyes. He had to remind himself again that she had just lost her husband. "How are you coping? I mean, other than having me springing the will on you, I can imagine the grief must be overwhelming."

Emma glanced at John, his green eyes filled with concern. She couldn't help but feel like a fraud. He was sympathizing without knowing the truth. She glanced toward the window and debated whether or not she should tell John the truth about her marriage to David. If he was just another *Englischer* Emma wouldn't even have considered it. But John wasn't, he used to be one of them. She returned her gaze to him and let out a heavy sigh. "John, there is something you should know about my marriage to David."

She could see the confusion clouding his eyes. "What is it, Emma?"

"Our marriage…" Emma swallowed past the lump that had formed in her throat and tried again. "We weren't a love match. My mother arranged for us to get married. Although I fought against it, I went along with it to appease her. I know you must think of me as weak and foolish, but it's the truth. So to be honest, I never loved David. We were only married for ninety-six days before he died."

John's eyebrows rose but he didn't say a word. He waited patiently for her to continue.

"It's not the grief that is overwhelming at the moment. Knowing that if I didn't marry David I wouldn't be sitting here with a pile of debt on my shoulders and a will that I don't understand…that's what is overwhelming me right now."

Emma let out a deep breath and shook her head. "So you see, my situation is rather unique."

John held her gaze as he mulled over the information in his mind. He wasn't even aware that arranged marriages were still happening in Amish communities, but apparently they did. The woman before him wasn't one grieving for the loss of her husband, but rather one grieving for the choices that had been made for her.

His heart swelled in his chest remembering her admission that she had never loved David Miller. She might be a widow, but she wasn't grieving. For some reason that made John feel better about the attraction he felt for her.

He reached across the table and touched her hand. "Emma, you are nothing if not unique." John had never been one for smooth words or affectionate touches but in that moment it felt right.

Their gazes held for a moment and without a doubt John knew that although Emma might deny it, she felt the connection between them as well. It was stronger than anything John had ever experienced before and frightened him more than anything else as well.

A notification from his cell phone interrupted the moment. He looked down at the screen and smiled. "We've spoken to Beatrice King," he said triumphantly.

"What did she say?" demanded Emma, pulling away her hand as if the moment never happened.

"I don't know, I've got to call her myself in about an hour," he said, reading the message. "She will be home then apparently."

"Well, it's a step forward," Emma said.

"Okay. I think it best that I do this in the motel. I might ask some uncomfortable questions, about David's past. It might be upsetting for you."

"I can't see how it will be given the situation. I hope what I've just told you won't influence your opinion of me," Emma said softly.

"Of course not, Emma. I'm sure there are many people who truly don't marry for love. You were doing what you felt was right. No one can blame you for that," John said, trying to make sure she felt better. "But I do think it's best that I make this call alone." *That way I won't be distracted by your smile or the way you flick that twirl of hair that peeks out from your* kapp, he thought. "I'll see you at the restaurant at nine thirty as planned."

"Fine, if you think that's best," smiled Emma. John's head spun again, and he drove back to the motel in a confused daze.

He stood up without saying another word and headed

outside, needing to clear the cobwebs from his mind and to figure out how he was going to solve this will without falling in love with the widow first.

Chapter Nine

The letters

The next morning Emma arose early preparing herself for a long day at the restaurant. She was meeting John for breakfast and she wanted to ensure that she looked nice. Although she knew pride was a terrible sin, she couldn't help herself. She wanted John to like her and looking nice was part of that. She ironed her apron and *kapp*, combed her hair, made adjustments here and there, and then finally decided she was as nice as she was going to look. Then she heard the familiar clip-clop of a buggy outside. Her heart sank. Her first thought was Eli King; he clearly hadn't taken the warning from John on board and here he was, about to serve her papers to get out of the house.

She looked out the window and saw Ruth climbing out clutching a fistful of documents.

Emma opened the door and embraced her sister. "Hi,

Ruth, this is a pleasant surprise, I was just about to walk to the restaurant. You only just caught me."

"Well I can drive you, it's on my way to work," Ruth replied. Ruth worked as a seamstress in a local tailoring shop. The owner employed her straight away when she applied for the position; she knew the Amish reputation for handwork and loyalty. She had been there for over five years now and as jobs go it wasn't a bad one. "Come on, I've some things to tell you, and something for you."

Emma grabbed her things and climbed into the buggy beside her sister. "So?" She said, waiting for the news.

Ruth handed Emma a bunch of old letters, stuffed in ripped envelopes. She pulled out the top one and immediately recognized David's handwriting.

"I found them last night, when I was sorting out Mother's things. They are letters to Mother, from David," said Ruth. "They are all about you."

"What?" asked Emma, confused.

"Look, I didn't read them all. I didn't think it was right. But from the few I read, it appears that David had been writing to Mother for some time. They were clearly trying to arrange a marriage between you two," replied Ruth.

"Really? How many letters?"

"I didn't count, but there were a lot. They start before you started working at the restaurant."

Emma remained silent; she didn't know what to say. "So they were manipulating me for all that time?" she finally said with anger. She knew that her mother had been keen on a match, but she didn't know it went as far back as this or that it seemed to be so organized.

Ruth reached out and touched her knee. "It might seem that way at the moment. But Emma, I think you need to read the letters before you make a judgment."

Emma looked at her sister, not understanding what she meant.

"Emma, just read them. Alone," repeated Ruth.

"Okay," she agreed, putting them into her bag and trying to dismiss them till she got to the restaurant.

"And I've got something exciting to tell you," said Ruth.

"Go on then. It seems to be the morning for news," replied Emma, still thinking about the letters.

Ruth's face lit up with delight. "Your handsome lawyer took me out for coffee yesterday and…"

"What?" exclaimed Emma, turning her head sharply to look at her sister.

"John Fisher, he took me out for coffee yesterday afternoon," replied Ruth slowly, as if Emma couldn't understand simple concepts.

"When?"

"I don't know, late afternoon sometime. Does it matter?" asked Ruth, not really expecting an answer to the question. "Anyway, guess what he said?" Again, there was no answer from her sister, who suddenly seemed to get very distant. She was looking at her, but not really seeing her. "Emma? Are you still with me?"

Emma's eyes seemed to regain focus. "No, tell me what he said," Emma whispered.

"Well, he gave no firm promise of course. But he

left enough hints that he would be interested in courting me."

"Did he?" Emma asked, very confused and hurt.
Last night she had experienced a connection with a man
for the first time. It was painful to imagine that only a
short while before that he had been taking her sister out.

"Isn't it exciting? I mean, I was beginning to think
there would never be someone for me," said Ruth, "Yet
here he could be."

Again Emma remained silent; not really understanding what was being said.

"Emma? Isn't it exciting?" Ruth said again. "What's
wrong with you this morning?"

Emma looked away to try hide her emotions from
her sister. How could she admit that she liked John? She
was newly widowed, and it would be frowned upon at
best. Her entire life was falling apart, her mother had
married her off as part of a cooked-up scheme and she
was stuck with a mountain of debt. How could Ruth ask
what was wrong with her?

Not for the first time she wished she and Ruth could
have been closer.

"Nothing, it's just that those letters have shocked
me, Ruth, that's all," said Emma, trying to show some
interest in what her sister was saying without revealing her real feelings. "How is all of this going to work,
Ruth? You're Amish, he's *Englisch*! He doesn't even
live around here."

"Oh, I have no idea. These are early days still," said
Ruth, completely ignoring some obvious practicalities.

"I'm pleased for you, Ruth, truly I am," smiled

Emma, although inside her heart felt anguish more than ever before. "Just be careful. Don't get hurt. Make sure that you understand what you might be getting yourself into. The *Englisch* are different to us."

Not that different to me, thought Ruth. She had already had two *Englisch* boyfriends when she was a teenager. Not that Emma or her mother ever knew that of course. She almost let it slip out that she was planning on leaving the community but held back at the last second. John had reminded her yesterday that Emma had lost everything over the last few months. She needed to be around for Emma at the moment. Everything must be hard for her. Ruth herself needed Emma at that moment. Losing their mother was hard, despite the fact that she and Ruth were never that close. She would take the big changes in her life steadily. But she knew she had to change them. "I'll be careful," Ruth insisted as they pulled up at the restaurant. "You read those letters, Emma. Please."

"I will," replied Emma, climbing down carefully. "*Denke*, see you soon." She ran inside before her sister could see the tears running down her face.

She crashed through the door and almost knocked down Stephanie who was carrying two mugs of coffee. "What's wrong?" she demanded, looking at the tears.

"Nothing! I just need a few minutes," replied Emma, going into the office and shutting the door behind her. She slumped in the office chair and cried. What was going on? She thought John was different, someone who she had a connection with. Turned out she had misread the situation completely and he was more interested in her sister. He didn't even tell her that he had taken her out for coffee. She laughed out loud at her stupidity. There was a soft knock on the office door and Stephanie's head appeared around the opening.

"Thought you might want a coffee," she said with a smile.

"Oh, *denke*, Stephanie," said Emma warmly, dabbing her eyes. "Don't worry," she continued, seeing the concern in the face of her friend. "I'm just being silly. I'll be all right in a minute."

"You sure?" asked Stephanie.

"*Jah*, I'm just going to take a little time to pull myself together, and then I'll be out to help," insisted Emma.

Stephanie just nodded and left her to it.

Emma decided to put all thoughts of John Fisher to the back of her mind. It was a stupid idea anyway. The arguments against a relationship with John that she had just presented to Ruth were equally valid to her.

Plus she had the added complication of being a widow. Obviously nothing could happen until a year had passed. She just felt a pang of pain that John seemed to have hidden all of this from her and she was sure that he experienced the same feelings she had the night before.

She could be wrong though. She was never good at reading signals from men. Emma pulled out the stack of letters that Ruth had given her, at a glance there must have been twenty of them at least. She began to take them all out of the envelopes and put them in chronological order. Fortunately, David seemed to have been taught the art of letter writing better than that of filing and all the letters were clearly dated.

The first one was written at least two months before she had started work in the restaurant. It seemed to be an introductory piece from David. In it he spoke about what a pleasure it was to attend church at our house that week, and how he had particularly enjoyed speaking to her after the service. Emma thought back and couldn't even remember a conversation taking place. She immediately felt guilty because of it. He said that he was very busy opening up a new business at present, but there was a matter he would like to speak to Mother about when they next met.

The second one seemed to be a follow up to the first. It was clear that the topic of the conversation that David wished to discuss had been her and that the two of them had done that at some length between the two letters. He wrote that he was delighted that Emma wasn't courting elsewhere and he was glad that Mother had seen no barrier to their age difference. He also insisted that he was honorable and had very true intentions and that he wouldn't do anything in the world to hurt her. Tears started welling up as Emma read. This was a man that barely knew her at this stage and here he was saying he wouldn't do anything in the world to hurt her.

Her mother had clearly sent a reply to this letter, because David wrote back in a little over a week. In the letter, he thanked her mother for her kind words and excellent suggestion. In it he said that Emma should apply for the position that was being advertised the normal way. But for Mother to be rest assured that she would be employed, he just wanted to make sure that it all seemed natural. He concluded the letter by saying how his world would be so enriched by working with Emma each day and how excited he was to get to know her better.

Emma didn't know how to feel. Part of her felt angry that she didn't even get the job here in the restaurant by her own skills, it was all part of their plotting. Yet another part of her felt sorrow and pain. David's devotion to her was so clear, and yet she knew nothing about it.

She read the letters and began to feel more guilty. It was clear that David was so in love with her and she had barely noticed him, other than as her boss. Her mother had clearly asked for regular updates on the position. At some point she must have commented to David about ensuring her daughters were married well, because David wrote back, saying that he would be the happiest man in the world if Emma were to agree to become his wife. Letter by letter she pieced together the plan. In one letter, David wrote that he was glad that her mother had now finally mentioned the idea of a marriage and that he was disappointed by Emma's initial reaction. Emma could not believe what she was reading, all the disagreements she had with her mother about her suggestion of a match with David had clearly all been reported to him.

And then there was the letter that finally left her stunned.

Bethany,

I denke *for the kind and encouraging words this Sunday. I confess that I was on the verge of giving up my pursuit of Emma, but your words have given me hope where there was none. A world without Emma is a world I would gladly depart. I know I have said so before, but you may rest assured that your daughter will be cared for beyond measure. I am fortunately a wealthy man; I have indicated some of the background in our conversations and see no need to repeat in writing. But I would like to impress you once more; I do not wish for Emma to be aware of these facts—not at this stage at least.*

I am realistic and grounded enough to see that Emma does not love me. With my great and growing love for her, understandably this pains me day to day. But I hope that with time Emma may grow to love me in the same way. I have prayed greatly on the matter and Gott *has shown me His will. I believe that our first year of marriage together (assuming of course that Emma ultimately agrees to honor me) will be a year spent in adversity.*

Gott *believes that I should show no indication of my wealth to Emma. I do not wish false affection to grow, although I doubt with Emma's sweet and caring nature that would happen. But* Gott *believes our love should grow without the burden of wealth to sway our human thoughts.*

I trust this is agreeable with you and I continue my renewed hope that soon I will be with the woman I love.

David.

The debt, the rented house, the lack of money. It was all part of David's plan for their first year of marriage together. David was not a stupid man; he obviously knew that Emma did not love him. But his grand scheme was that affection and love would grow as they fought against money problems. She shook her head. Poor David, he was clearly so in love with her that he would resort to anything to attempt to get her to love him back. He had died without that ever happening and Emma felt nothing but guilt and regret.

She sat back and for a few moments allowed herself to wonder what life might have been like if David had lived. Would she have grown to love him? Would she have been able to return the deep affection he had so clearly felt for her?

Another knock at the door caused her to jump. Stephanie appeared with a big beaming smile on her face. "Your handsome lawyer is here," she said excitedly.

"I see," said Emma, not sharing the same enthusiasm. "Tell him to wait, will you."

Stephanie raised her eyebrows but disappeared to deliver the message.

Emma grabbed the pile of letters and arranged them neatly. Now, what was she going to do about John Fisher?

Chapter Ten

Misunderstanding

John had endured a long night. His phone call with David Miller's sister was enlightening and he had some answers for Emma about her husband's past. He'd also managed to get an address for the farm bequeathed to Beatrice in the will. Or at least, if Beatrice's suspicions were correct it was the right address. Then he was hit by a series of emails and phone calls from Karl Seymour.

In light of the new evidence and its associated media coverage, Seymour had decided to request that the trial be moved. His belief was that the hit man-hiring teacher couldn't get a fair trial in Cleveland. But there was research that had to be done for the submission. John had a laptop and an internet connection, Seymour made sure that he did his share of the task, even if he was in Holmes County.

The more he worked and the more he went through the new evidence, the less he found he liked the firm's client. As Seymour had made clear, this new evidence was strong. A fair trial probably wasn't available in Cleveland.

John didn't voice his opinion on the matter since he didn't believe that the client deserved a fair trial. He had spent the morning wondering if this was what the rest of his life was going to be like. Was he going to be flogging himself by working eighteen hour days to defend sleazeballs just to fatten his bank account?

What happened to integrity? What happened to justice? It seemed the longer he was a lawyer, the more he learned that any crime could be excused as long as you had enough influence, power and money to throw around.

He studied law because he wanted to make a difference for the victims, not the criminals that deserved a dark cell without sunlight for the rest of their lives.

It was hard to admit his life had come down to this. He shoved the thought aside and finally headed to bed.

His last thought before he drifted off was that tomorrow he was buying breakfast for a beautiful woman, who wanted nothing materialistic from him at all. It was a refreshing change from the previous women in his life. Women who had been drawn to him not for his personality and character, but for his looks and the fact that he was a highly paid lawyer. He closed his eyes and dreamt of Emma Miller.

When Emma greeted him that morning with a cold "Good morning, Mr. Fisher," John immediately knew something was wrong. Her eyes were hard and her composure as stiff as a board.

She joined him at the table, not relaxing even the least bit.

"Do you have any news?" she asked as if last night had never happened.

John shifted uncomfortably in his seat, feeling as if he had imagined the moment they had shared. "I've got some news about Beatrice Miller that I'll explain in a minute. But it's all good so there is no need to worry. What's excellent on here, then?"

"It's all good," said Emma, without the hint of a smile. "My husband always made sure that everything we sold was of the finest quality."

John attempted to ignore the arctic breeze that had joined the table. Maybe Emma simply didn't feel so comfortable around him when in public. He thought she might warm up after eating. Stephanie came over to take their order.

John spoke first. "Eggs Benedict please. Then I think I'll go for some pancakes."

"Juice?" Stephanie asked jotting everything down on her ordering pad.

"No, just coffee for me please, Stephanie," replied a grinning John as Stephanie scratched down his order on her pad. "Emma?"

Emma looked up at Stephanie and gave her a smile, "Just coffee for me please, Stephanie, I won't be eating."

The server nodded and bustled away to the kitchen with the order.

"You're not eating today, Emma, is something wrong?" asked John softly, reaching out and touching her arm.

She immediately pulled it back out of John's reach. "I think we need to get a few things straight, Mr. Fisher," said Emma, in her best "don't mess with me in my restaurant" voice. She'd had to deal with a few drunks in the evenings before and she fell back on this approach.

John frowned and sat back, giving her a little distance. "All right?"

"I do not appreciate you courting my sister instead of attending to the matter at hand."

"Courting your sister?" John asked baffled. "I'm sorry, I've lost you."

"Ruth told me that you had a date yesterday. Although that is none of my business, I want to remind you the purpose of your visit to Holmes County."

John stiffened slightly before a grin broke on his face. Clearly Ruth had embellished their brief coffee but what intrigued him more was Emma's reaction. Was she jealous? Could it be that he hadn't imagined the moment they had shared the night before?

With his smile in place he held her gaze. "Yeah, I bought Ruth a coffee yesterday, and yes, in the middle of everything else I forgot to mention it last night. But it was hardly planned."

"That's not how Ruth told it."

"I'll be sure to run any coffee meetings I have by you while I'm in Holmes County." He chuckled and tilted his head a little. Did Emma even know that although she was trying her best to remain professional it was clear she was jealous? "I was heading out of the storage place yesterday while looking at my phone and not paying the slightest attention to where I was going. Ruth was coming the other way and I simply went straight through her. I didn't see her till I'd knocked her to the floor."

"So it wasn't a date?" Emma said, her resolve slowly fizzing out.

"No, she seemed a little shaky. Like I mentioned, I completely knocked her to the ground. I offered to buy her a coffee and just stay with her for a few minutes until I saw that she was going to be all right. I didn't want to just say sorry and rush off."

"Oh," Emma said slightly less sure of her ground.

John shook his head, even more bemused than before. "It was a chance encounter. I couldn't just leave her there, could I? I had to make sure she was okay."

"That was very kind of you," Emma said quietly, her gaze glued to the table.

John lowered his voice and glanced around to make sure no one was in earshot before he spoke again. "Let me make this perfectly clear, Emma, I'm not interested in Ruth. If I was interested in anyone at the moment it wouldn't matter, because she just buried her husband."

John didn't know why he had said that, but the words had escaped him before he could stop.

Emma glanced up and met his gaze with a startled expression. "What did you just say?"

A slow smile spread across John's face. "You heard me, but like I said, it doesn't matter because nothing can come from it. You're my client…" he let the words trail off for her to fill in the rest.

She was an Amish widow and he was *Englisch*. Even if he wanted more or wanted to pursue the connection they had shared the night before, it wouldn't be possible.

Emma slowly nodded with a sigh, understanding just as he knew she would. His gaze softened. "Another time, another life...sometimes fate just likes to tease us with possibilities, doesn't it?"

Emma sighed. "You're right, fate can be infuriating. I'm sorry for my behavior earlier. It was uncalled for. You have every right to see who you choose to see."

"And I don't choose to see anyone except my client at this moment." John chuckled wryly. "Perhaps I should see your sister just to make sure we're on the same page. Next thing I know she'll be planning a wedding."

"Don't think badly of her, John. She has always been the same. Ruth has a great love for the *Englisch* world. She's had *Englisch* boyfriends before now. She thinks that my mother and I didn't know. But we did. She would talk to me about leaving the community, more than once, and if I'm honest, now that poor Mother has passed, I don't think it will be long before she does."

John nodded, wanting to tell Emma that her instincts were right. But he had promised Ruth that what she told him would go no further, so he kept his mouth shut. "Perhaps you're right. So, Emma? Are we all right again now? Are you going to drop this Mr. Fisher stuff?"

Emma went bright red, just like the first time he saw her. "Okay, John, tell me about David's sister."

Stephanie suddenly appeared with the food and slapped it down on the table. "That looks good," said John.

"Indeed it does," agreed Emma, looking up at Stephanie. "I've changed my mind. A plate of pancakes for me, please."

Stephanie grinned, pleased that her friend seemed better and rushed off to prepare it.

John spoke as he ate. "So, Beatrice Miller hadn't spoken to her brother in about nine years. She was very shocked when our paralegal told her that her brother had died and under such tragic circumstances. She told me that she regretted not now having the opportunity to make up for lost time with him."

Emma could understand that, she made a note that whatever Ruth decided about her future the two of them must never fall out to the degree that they lose contact. She would hate to ever be in Beatrice Miller's position; a phone call out of the blue from someone you don't know to tell you your sister had died. It brought a shudder to her spine.

"It turns out that you seemed to already know the basics of what happened. Beatrice decided during her *Rumspringa* that she didn't want to be baptized. There was a big fallout over it all. Apparently David tried to be the peacemaker between their parents and her, and to get them to understand, but they said they never would. Beatrice caught the three of them talking about how David could try to persuade her to stay and that resulted in a big fallout between the two siblings. She exploded, telling David that he was siding with them."

John chewed his breakfast thoughtfully. "I've seen less drama on soap operas on television, to be honest." Emma stared back, not understanding the joke. "Sorry, not a reference you would understand."

He continued, "Anyway, that turned out to be the last conversation the two of them ever had. She packed her bags and disappeared with nothing more than seventy-five dollars in her pocket. The parents disowned her, and she found out from a friend that she still had in the community that they had left the family farm to David. She only found out about her parents when it was too late, so she didn't even make it to the funeral. You know how they died, don't you?"

"To be honest, I don't," said Emma, thinking that the subject of how David's parents died never came up in their conversations.

"It was a buggy accident just like David's."

Emma sat in silence for a moment. "Shocking. I mean who would have thought it was possible?"

"The world can be a very strange place at times," agreed John.

"I'm guessing that the farm in Missouri is the family farm that his parents left him?"

"Got it in one!" smiled John. "Beatrice doesn't know what she will end up doing with it. She's a tailor now, runs a small shop and is very happy with her life apparently. She never married, well, not yet anyway. She came close once or twice. She's dating a nice man at the moment, who's a teacher, she said. But she was glad that David had managed to find happiness in his life, if only for a short while."

The words hit home to Emma. They confirmed what had been said in the letters to her mother. By agreeing to marry him, Emma realized that she had made David happy. And for that, now she felt glad.

"So at least I have the address and details on one of the properties. Of course, until I see the deed documents, I'm not going to be one hundred percent sure," said John. "Now all we have to do is find them all."

Emma shrugged her shoulders. "I'm lost now. I don't know where to look next. I've looked everywhere I can think of. Unless he has a lockbox in a bank somewhere or I start cutting open the mattresses, I can't think of another way to find them."

"Well, we gotta find them. My boss is expecting me back in the office in the morning," replied John, standing up and excusing himself.

Stephanie brought over Emma's pancakes as John disappeared into the restroom. She began eating and her eyes fell on the pile of letters from David. She didn't even realize that she had brought them out with her. She hadn't finished going through them yet. Her eyes scanned the last unread letter on the top, then suddenly she froze and pushed away her plate. She picked up the letter and read in more detail and gave out a triumphant cry!

John emerged from the restroom and Emma leapt to her feet. "Come on," she shouted. "I know where the deeds are!"

Chapter Eleven

The answer

"No wait, we have to go and see Ruth first!" shouted Emma as John sped off in the wrong direction.

"What? Why? I don't think that's a good idea," said John, thinking about Emma's revelations earlier.

Emma smiled mischievously. "Afraid she's going to propose? Don't worry, you can wait in the car. Turn right over there," Emma ordered with a glint in her eye.

John simply did as he was told. Five minutes later he was pulling up outside a tailor's shop and Emma had the door open before he had even stopped moving.

She ran inside and looked for her sister. Ruth was shocked to see her. "What's wrong?" she demanded, immediately thinking that something was amiss.

"No, everything is good. Or at least I hope everything is good. Those letters you gave me, where did you find them?"

"In with Mother's papers. Why?" Ruth questioned, confused by the thread of the conversation.

"Were there any other papers with them?" Emma pressed, grasping her sister's hand in the excitement.

"Yes, hundreds of papers. You know Mother! Everything from her first store receipt right up to the infomercial pamphlets that come in the mail."

Emma certainly did know her mother; she never threw a thing out. She always insisted that you never know when you might need something. That is was why she was paying for a storage unit full of junk; she simply couldn't bear to let anything go.

"Where are the rest of the papers?" asked Emma, praying silently that Ruth hadn't thrown them away.

"I've put them all in a massive cardboard box on the dining room table. My plan was to sort through them this week. I saw the letters straight away and was intrigued. Did you read them?"

"Oh yes! I read them," said Emma, already running for the door. "*Denke*, Ruth. Love you! I'll see you later, hopefully with some good news."

She slipped back into the car and smiled at John. "We've got a massive cardboard box to search through! Come on, let's get moving!"

John slipped the car into Drive and pulled away.

It didn't take long to reach the house. As they came to Emma's house she suddenly shouted, "Stop!" John slammed on his brakes and looked around as though there was a mysterious hidden rider somewhere that he hadn't seen.

"Wait here," she commanded and ran into her house.

She emerged after less than two minutes with a large basket. She climbed back inside, and the aroma of fresh bread hit John's nostrils. He looked at Emma inquisitively.

"Trust me! We are going to be at Ruth's house. She won't have food! My sister lives off preprepared stuff she buys from the supermarket up the road from the tailor's. And I know my mother, there is going to be a lot of paperwork to go through." She held up the basket. "We are going to need sustenance."

It took them another five minutes to reach Ruth's house. Emma found the key, still hidden in the normal spot, and as they entered she suddenly realized this was the first time she had been there since their mother died. She thought for a moment about how much had changed in such a short period of time. Once the matter of the will was resolved Emma vowed to have some quiet time and reflect on where her life was and to give thanks for the good things that had been in it.

Emma pulled out the letter to her mother from David. She flattened it out carefully on the table and read out loud the appropriate passage.

"I appreciate your concerns. I know you approve of my plan to forge love out of a common adversity, but I understand your need to be assured that this adversity is not real. We have discussed at length my finances, but I wish for you to have peace of mind before the wedding next week (I can hardly believe I am writing those words...)"

Emma gulped and tried to control her emotions before reading out the next line.

"(Your daughter will make me the happiest and most joyful man alive. God willing.) I enclose the deeds to the property I discussed with you, together with the statements from the bank that handles the lease income. You will see that everything I told you is true and just. I request that you keep these documents in a safe place until I request them from you; I should not wish Emma to stumble on them by accident. I want to be able to explain the reasons for my actions at the appropriate time without her believing I have kept things from her."

Emma looked at John, who was shaking his head in disbelief. "So the documents are here! I don't understand what David was trying to achieve?"

"There was a whole pile of letters to my mother, John. A whole pile. It was clear that he loved me more than any woman deserves to be loved. I was not worthy of such love." She sat down, her head awash with anguish and regret. She wished she could thank David for his devotion. She wished she had the opportunity to love him back the way he had loved her. But it was not to be.

"David knew I didn't love him. And he didn't want me just marrying him and loving him because of money." She gave out a little laugh. "Not that I would do that anyway. But I'm sure some girls do. David wanted me to grow to love him as we battled these problems together."

"I see," said John, nodding his head. "Obviously David never expected your mother to pass so quickly and therefore the documents should still be here."

Emma nodded. "Or rather the documents should be in there!" She pointed to a very large cardboard box that was full to the brim with papers.

At first glance it looked like an intimidating task. But John was a lawyer who was used to working through papers quickly and he immediately took charge. "Emma, you make us some coffee, I'll start going through this. Remember I know what I'm looking for."

By the time Emma had returned with the mugs of coffee, John was clutching some papers with a beaming face. "Congratulations!" he said, handing Emma the documents.

The property deeds meant little to Emma; they just had addresses on them and pages of legal talk that she didn't understand. But she could immediately see that there were deeds for the number of properties mentioned in David's will. She then unfolded the bank statements and let out a gasp of surprise. She felt light-headed and sat down, then looked at John waving the statement in the air. He simply smiled at her. "I guess Eli King is going to have his rent paid to him for a while!"

Chapter Twelve

Bitter regret

John's smile quickly faded when he noticed the ashen look on Emma's face. He kneeled down in front of her and took her hand before he looked into her eyes, "Breathe, Emma, this is good news."

Emma nodded but there wasn't a smile or look of relief in sight. Instead, it looked as if she was about to faint. "All this time… All this time I thought we were poor, barely scraping by and now to see this…" Emma let out a heavy sigh and shook her head. "I'm relieved knowing that I don't have that debt resting on my shoulders, but also I can't help but feeling betrayed."

John nodded. "If it's any consolation, I think they planned this out of love. Your mother wanted the best for you and judging by these documents, David was a good man, a wealthy man at that. Rather think of what their scheming could mean for you, instead of thinking about the betrayal."

"You're right. I'm being foolish again."

John chuckled softly as he met her gaze. "You could never be foolish, Emma Miller, even if you tried."

She looked over the documents in her hand again, leafing through them one by one before finally looking up into John's gaze again. John had achieved what he had come to Holmes County to do, but victory was bittersweet. Because finding the deeds meant it was time for him to go back to Cleveland. He had no reason to stay in Holmes County for another minute but as he looked into Emma's eyes, he couldn't help but wish they hadn't found the deeds for a few days yet.

He squeezed her hand and carefully stood up, before he walked to the window. A thick silence hung in the house, thick enough that it could be cut with a dull blade.

John cleared the emotion from his throat, surprised at how little he looked forward to going back to Cleveland. He had come to Holmes County on the request of his employer and had dreaded coming back to the place he had left behind so many years before, but now the thought of leaving again was even harder.

Because this time it wouldn't just be leaving behind the memories of his Amish childhood, he would be leaving behind the first woman that had ever touched his heart. Although no declarations of love were made and neither of them admitted to the feelings that they had for each other or the connection they had shared, John didn't doubt either for a moment.

Just once, John wished that he didn't have to get back to work or go back to all the responsibilities he had in

Cleveland. What he wouldn't have given to spend a few more days in Holmes County. He wanted to get to know Emma, wanted to spend more time with her and to explore the connection they had.

But that was a dream and it was time John faced reality again. He turned around and saw Emma had pulled herself together and placed the deeds on the table. She sat with her hands folded in her lap and looked at him with a questioning look. "What happens now?"

"Now that we found the deeds, everything is a lot simpler. I need to get back to Cleveland to make sure all the right channels are followed to put everything in your name. I'll try my best to get you access to the bank accounts as soon as possible. I'm sure as soon as you can repay some of that debt and get Eli King off your shoulders you'll feel a lot better." John's voice sounded cool to his own ears. It was the professional tone he used with his clients, with whom he kept an emotional distance.

"So you'll be heading back right now?" Emma's voice was neutral, the shadows had returned to her gaze.

John almost said yes, hoping that if he left right now he could forget all about Emma Miller and her hazel eyes that made his heart beat faster. But that wasn't the way it worked. "I'll need copies of your identity documents. I'll head into town and scan and email them over to my office before returning them to you. If it's all right with you, I'll come back early afternoon after checking out of my motel and then I'll be heading back to Cleveland."

"*Denke*, John," Emma said softly.

John nodded and clenched his jaw. Although he was coming back again this afternoon, he knew that Emma's thank you sounded like a goodbye because that's what it was. Whatever they had shared in these past few days would be nothing but a memory tomorrow. "I'm glad I could've been of assistance."

Emma nodded before heading to her purse. A few moments later she returned giving him two identity documents. As John took the documents their hands brushed, reminding him of what he will be leaving behind.

"I know you feel betrayed by your mother and David, but I can understand why he would've gone through so much trouble to have you, he was a very lucky man in the end."

John turned and collected the deeds from the dining room table before he let himself out. The sooner he reminded himself who and what he was, the better. There is no place in an Amish widow's life for an *Englisch* lawyer, just like Cleveland was no place for an Amish woman.

Chapter Thirteen

A tearful goodbye

After John left, Emma gave herself some time to work through all the emotions buzzing around in her mind. After almost an hour she finally collected her things, locked up Ruth's home and headed to her home. She let herself into the home she had shared with David and as soon as she stepped inside she realized she wouldn't move. Now that she had enough money to secure rent, she couldn't imagine sharing a house with Ruth again.

She might not have loved David, but over the last three months his house had become her home. He had given her the freedom to move the furniture as she preferred it, to organize the pantry in a way that suited her and didn't even balk when she had covered the bed with the pastoral blue and pink quilt she had made as a young lady.

A tear slipped over her cheek realizing that David giving her the freedom to make changes to his house had been his way of making her feel at home. She couldn't help but regret that she hadn't known of his strong feelings for her earlier. Would she have done something differently? A heavy sigh escaped her as she admitted to herself that although David was a very kind man, he had never made her heart skip a beat and that they had never shared the connection that she had experienced with John, whom she barely knew.

If it hadn't been for those letters, she would've never known how David had felt about her.

She wouldn't have known that the financial struggles had been his way of getting her to fall in love with him. Emma wanted to be angry at her mother, but after reading the letters she could admit her mother was only acting in her best interest, even if her perception was a little skewed.

She headed to the kitchen to brew herself a fresh pot of tea, hoping her mother's belief that tea soothes any ache would help. She settled with a cup of tea at the dining room table and began packing out all the papers she had collected from the box of her mother's. After placing the bank statements on top of each other, she headed to a room to collect the calculator that David kept there to tally up the sales from the restaurant. There were three bank accounts: one for lease payments, one for investments, and one for savings. By the time she added up all the amounts she couldn't believe the number of zeros on the small screen. Her heart raced in her chest knowing that the debt the restaurant had incurred wouldn't even remove a drop from the bucket of wealth she now owned.

John had been right; Emma might be a widow, but she was a very wealthy widow. A small smile played on her mouth as she thought of Eli King and what his reaction was going to be if she gave him a years' rent up front. No, she corrected herself, she wouldn't be that kind or give him that satisfaction; she would give him six months' rent up front.

When she heard a car pull up outside she was surprised to see that four hours had passed since she arrived home. It was hard to believe everything that she had uncovered between David's papers. The properties were leased for enough money every month, even without the restaurant, Emma never had to work another day in her life. She pushed the papers aside and headed to the front door when she heard John's footsteps on the porch. She opened the door and she was faced once again with a man she couldn't bear to say goodbye to.

John had changed into a pair of jeans and a white shirt and wore sunglasses. He was clearly ready to head back to Cleveland. The thought made her stomach drop to her feet. "I see you're ready to get on the road?"

John nodded as he held out the identity documents. "Yes, the sooner I get this sorted for you the better."

Emma nodded excepting the documents. "*Denke* for bringing these back."

"I'll be in touch. Can I call you at the restaurant, or leave a message for you there?"

"Yes, that would be fine, *denke*."

John nodded and although the business was dealt with, he didn't move to leave. Instead, he stood on the porch

searching Emma's eyes. She wondered if he was searching for the same thing she was; a reason for him to stay.

After a few moments he finally let out a sigh and
held out his hand in a formal way. "It was a pleasure
to meet you, Mrs. Miller. I wish you all the best in the
future." The greeting was so formal that Emma could
feel the tears burn the back of her eyes. She bit them
back and shook his hand. "*Denke* for your trouble, Mr.
Fisher. I'll be forever grateful to you."

John nodded once before he turned and headed back
to his car. Emma stood on the porch and folded her
hands over her chest as if to protect herself from the
heartache she knew would come when she watched him
drive away.

She wanted to regret ever marrying David Miller,
but as she watched John's taillights grow smaller in the
distance, she knew she couldn't. Not only had David left
her a mountain of wealth, but if it hadn't been for him
she would've never met John Fisher. Although nothing had come from their brief connection, Emma knew
she would never forget the handsome *Englisch* lawyer.

Chapter Fourteen

A rude awakening

Pascal and Seymour were both overjoyed when John walked into the office shortly before six o'clock that evening. Most people in the city were heading home to start dinner and to spend some time with family and friends, but at their law firm it was considered slacking if you left before eight o'clock.

In his years at the firm, John had seen numerous associates overlooked for promotion because they had a good work-life balance.

"Everything sorted out in Holmes County?" Seymour asked with a cocked brow as he followed John into his office. After setting down his briefcase John turned to Seymour with a reserved smile before holding up the deeds.

"I have the deeds as well as the bank account numbers of all David Miller's personal accounts. Mrs. Miller is going to be a very wealthy widow."

"Good, good. I'm glad to hear it. We'll get a paralegal to deal with that. I need you to dig into the other case. There's been a few developments." Seymour let out a heavy groan indicating the developments were not good. "A witness has stepped forward. The prosecutor won't reveal who the witness is for his own protection but that is never a good thing."

John nodded. "I'll get on it." The words flowed from his mouth automatically but as soon as Seymour smiled and left his office he regretted them. The further this case went on, the more John realized he didn't want to defend Seymour's friend. Nothing about this case seemed right. The man was guilty as sin and yet Seymour was pulling all resources to defend him.

He glanced down at the papers in his hand and decided not to hand them over to a paralegal after all. He would make sure everything in David's will was handled efficiently himself, even if that meant putting in the extra hours.

After calling his assistant, he briefed her on what he needed her to do to get the bank accounts put in Emma's name. He could see the question in her eyes because he was handling such a menial matter, but he didn't explain himself to her.

Instead he collected his things and headed home. It was only seven o'clock, but he needed fresh air and a reality check to get him back into the right frame of mind to start on Seymour's case again in the morning. The street was buzzing with families and couples heading to the store or heading out for dinner, but all John could see was how far removed Cleveland was from Holmes

County. The technology, the noise, the rush, and the stressed expressions on the faces of passersby were all just another reminder that life was different in the city.

He stopped in at the pizza place he frequented and ordered his usual; pepperoni with extra olives and mozzarella. A short while later he was walking to his apartment with a hot pizza and wishing he was anywhere else but in Cleveland.

As soon as he stepped into his apartment, he realized that, although he had lived there for the last five years, it didn't feel like home. In fact, it was just a place where he laid his head when he was tired and to work late when he didn't feel like being at the office. He didn't even own a dining room table. Suddenly his appetite vanished when he remembered the meal Emma had cooked for him. Why couldn't he cook like that?

Because he didn't have the time, he admitted to himself with a heavy sigh. He opened the box and took out a slice more out of habit than hunger and bit into the cheesy dough. He waited for the flavor to explode in his mouth but instead it tasted the same as it always did. A quick meal for a rushed man who had more important things on his mind.

Tonight, those more important things weren't related to his career, they were related to one client: Emma Miller.

He tossed the piece of pizza back into the box and headed to his room instead. After a quick shower he headed to bed without even bothering to switch on the air conditioning or the television. He had gotten used to the quiet of the country and tonight the sounds of the city kept him awake.

He wouldn't admit that it was the face of an Amish widow that haunted his thoughts, because that would be admitting to losing his heart to a woman in just a few short days who he could never have.

By the time he drifted off to sleep his dreams were filled with images of a home in the country and a beautiful Amish wife. There were two little kids playing in the yard as the white sheets danced in the breeze. There wasn't any noise from the cars rushing past or police racing to catch a criminal. Instead, there was only the sound of Emma's laughter and the bees buzzing over the spring blooms. He woke up shortly after midnight covered in a cold sweat because he knew that dream was the most appealing he had ever had.

Chapter Fifteen

White elephants need to be faced

Three weeks.

It had been three weeks since Emma said goodbye to John, and four weeks since burying David. And although her friends, her sister, and the community were offering her all the support she needed, Emma had never felt more alone.

Things between her and Ruth had been stilted since John's visit to Holmes County.

Neither sister had mentioned the handsome lawyer again, but the tension was palpable between them. Of course, they had to see each other to discuss their mother's estate, which proved more awkward than ever before.

Although Emma knew that she had no claim on John or who he dated, she couldn't help but feel that in typical Ruth-style her sister had moved in like a vulture at the most inappropriate time. It was just like Ruth to always think of herself and what she wanted without considering whether or not it was appropriate.

Emma had invited Ruth for dinner, hoping to finally break the ice and rescue their relationship. She knew that Ruth could be stubborn when she wanted to and could only hope that Ruth wouldn't be so tonight.

In an effort to win her sister's friendship, and hopefully repair a relationship that had never been whole in the first place, Emma had made Ruth's favorite dinner: spaghetti.

Although John had promised to stay in touch, Emma hadn't heard from him again. She went to the restaurant on most days, and always double checked for messages. To date, John hadn't tried once to reach her.

Despite knowing that she could afford to pay off the debt, she couldn't help but become anxious about finally having access to David's bank accounts. The sooner she paid off the loans and the suppliers that sent a steady stream of final notices, the sooner the reality of her wealth could start sinking in. At the moment she still felt like a penniless widow with the wolves baying at the door.

When there was a knock at the door, Emma was grateful that Ruth was on time. She was a little concerned about how their dinner would go, but she was hopeful that it would go well.

"Hello, Ruth," Emma said as she opened the door with a broad smile.

Ruth didn't smile as she stepped inside. "Hello, Emma." A frown creased Ruth's brow as she turned to face Emma. "Do I smell spaghetti?" she asked with a hopeful grin.

"*Jah*, you do. I was hoping it would make you smile."

The sisters walked into the kitchen together, where Emma served them each a glass of juice, after which they sat down at the table. They spoke about unimportant things for a short while, and Emma didn't mind because she knew that this was their way of finding equal ground. The conversation turned to their mother's estate, and what they would be keeping and what they would sell.

When Ruth let out a heavy sigh and searched Emma's face, Emma couldn't help but feel slightly uncomfortable. "Is something wrong, Ruth?"

"Even if there was, it wouldn't matter," Ruth said dejectedly.

Emma frowned, wondering why her sister believed her problems didn't matter. "Of course it matters, you're my *schweschder*. It matters to me if something's wrong."

Ruth gave a wry chuckled. "I'm just looking at you and wondering why *Mamm* decided to find you a match and never bothered to find one for me?"

Emma opened her mouth but quickly closed it again, not knowing how to answer.

"I always knew you were her favorite, but now I can't help but wonder if she loved you more as well?"

Emma reached for her sister's hand and squeezed it tightly. "That's absurd. She didn't love me more; we got along well because we were more alike."

"So, I was different?"

Emma smiled patiently. "Ruth, if *Mamm* had arranged a match for you, you wouldn't have gone along with it, would you?"

The sad expression fled from her sister's gaze as a smile blossomed. "*Nee*, you're right. I wouldn't have."

Emma chuckled. "See, then you've got nothing to be jealous about. Besides, if I hadn't found those deeds, I would've been a very poor widow with nothing but debt."

"I'm glad you aren't. That way I wouldn't have to worry when…" Ruth trailed off and Emma suddenly felt a strange feeling come over her.

"When what, Ruth?" Emma questioned, afraid that she already knew what the answer was going to be."

"Emma, you know that I've never loved this simple life. Even as a little girl you would bask in its simplicity while I yearned to wear *Englisch* dresses and have *Englisch* dolls," Ruth said quietly as a tear slipped over her cheek.

Emma felt her heart clench in her chest. Nothing Ruth said was surprising to her, after all. She had been expecting to have this conversation with her sister for years, but the reality of it all made her feel sad.

"I know, Ruth. Have you made a decision?" Emma asked carefully.

Ruth nodded. "I've been thinking this over ever since *Mamm* passed. At first, I tried to ignore it, knowing I couldn't leave you, especially since we only have each other now. But Emma, I don't think I'll ever be happy here. If I don't leave, I know I'll regret it for the rest of my life. I can't stay…" Ruth trailed off and Emma drew in a sharp breath knowing she was about to lose another person she loved.

"You've been baptized, Ruth…if you leave, it would be akin to shunning. The bishop won't let you come back."

Ruth sighed with a sad smile. "That's what made the decision so hard. I know I won't be able to come back. But, Emma…do you really think I would be happy if I stayed?"

Emma shook her head; she didn't answer because she knew Ruth would never find the joy in their simple life that Emma had cherished for so many years.

"I've sorted out all *Mamm*'s things. The storage room is almost empty, you can just go take a look if there's anything you'd like to keep before I sell the rest. As for the furniture… I won't be taking any with me, so if there's something you'd like to keep, I'll help you bring it here. I'm not renewing the lease on the *haus*, Emma. I will leave when the lease comes to an end in a few weeks. That will give me enough time to decide where I want to go. I was thinking of Cleveland, perhaps."

Emma's eyes flew up to meet her sister's, surprised to find a teasing look on Ruth's face. "I knew that would've caught your attention," Ruth teased. "I don't know where I'm going yet, but I know I'm going."

Emma sighed. "Then we had better enjoy dinner because I don't think we have many left together."

Ruth stood up and hugged her younger sister. Emma could understand how hard this decision must have been for Ruth, not that is was the least bit easy for her either. She was losing another person after she had already lost so much. She would never even consider becoming *Englisch* or leaving the community, but it still hurt to know her sister was going to search for a life far away from her.

When Ruth pulled back, she searched Emma's gaze. "Will you give me the recipe before I leave?"

Emma smiled. "Of course I'll give you the recipe. *Mamm* had all her recipes written down in a book. If you like, you can take that as well. I know it will come in handy."

"I'd appreciate it. Thank you."

Emma nodded before she reached for two plates and began serving the spaghetti. Now she understood why she hadn't seen that much of Ruth. While she had been so caught up with her own situation, her sister had been dealing with a situation of her own.

The tension of earlier was gone by the time Emma washed the dishes. They enjoyed a cup of tea and discussed what still needed to be done before Ruth could board a bus out of Holmes County. By the time Ruth left for home, Emma didn't bother heading back inside. She allowed the tears she had bitten back over dinner to fall. They streamed down her face in quiet rivulets as she watched the stars in the night sky.

Chapter Sixteen

A personal delivery

It was Friday morning and, as usual, John was at work before most of the office workers had even enjoyed their first cup of coffee. After checking his emails, he glanced at the paperwork his assistant had placed on his desk the day before.

A sigh escaped him as he leaned back in his chair. The folder filled with papers taunted him from the corner of his table. It was a needless reminder of the widow he couldn't stop thinking about. Although finalizing a will could take up to a year in some cases, that of David Miller was moving along smoothly. It had taken a little longer than he expected, but all the bank accounts were finally signed over into Emma's name.

In most cases that's where the firm's responsibility would have ended, but John had made sure that a paralegal applied for new checkbooks as well. Emma would finally be able to pay off the debt David had left her in.

As soon as she received the package on John's desk, that is. Normally, a hand-to-hand courier would be used to deliver such important documents, but for some reason John hadn't asked his assistant to arrange for one.

It was the weekend after Labor Day, and most of the staff were taking a long weekend and the opportunity to soak up the last dredges of summer before winter set in, but John had made no such plans. The thought of spending the weekend on a beach somewhere didn't appeal to him in the least. Holmes County was a different story altogether.

A small smile grazed his face as he thought about the hand-to-hand courier. Perhaps, instead of spending the weekend at home or alone in the office, he could head to Holmes County to deliver the documents personally. With the wheels now turning in his mind, John remembered his promise to stay in touch with Emma after his return to Cleveland. He hadn't contacted her once since he arrived back. Not only was he overwhelmed with the case Seymour had assigned him to, he had also tried his best to push Emma from his mind.

Every time more evidence came to light, it was clear that Seymour's friend didn't deserve a defense. What defense could there be for a hit man-hiring teacher who dealt drugs to students?

The connection he had felt with Emma remained with him, and when he first returned John had believed keeping his distance and not contacting her would somehow make him forget what he had felt during the few short days in Holmes County. But forgetting Emma was impossible. She was the first woman that had ever made John think of the future; she had made him re-assess his whole life and he couldn't help but admit it came up short. His life was filled with goals, ambitions, and wealth and had none of the real wealth of Emma's life. Wealth in the sense of family, faith, and loyalty. It didn't matter how hard he tried to convince himself that what he felt for Emma was merely sympathy, John knew it wasn't.

It was so much more.

He knew he couldn't act on the attraction he felt for Emma, regardless of her being a widow. She was Amish. But every night when he went to bed, it was her face that came to mind.

There was still the matter of the deeds that needed to be transferred into her name, that had been handed over to the deeds office. But other than that, the para-legals had achieved in a matter of weeks what usually would take months.

Apart from the healthy bank accounts, they had also discovered a life insurance policy that David had taken out in the event of his death. John also had news to share with her. An appointment with his client would be in order and wouldn't be frowned upon by the part-ners; the only problem was that John wasn't going to expect Emma to come all the way to Cleveland to meet with him.

No, he was going to see her.

He was going back to Holmes County.

Excitement started pulsing in his veins at the thought of seeing her again. He glanced at the documents one last time before turning to his computer. The sooner he dealt with his duties for the day and answered a few emails regarding the case he was working on for Seymour, he could hit the road. If all went well, he could be in Holmes County by this evening.

By the time his assistant arrived at work, John was already knee-deep into his day's responsibilities. He lost track of time as he handled a few matters for Pascal and by the time lunchtime rolled around he was almost ready to pack up. He wished his assistant a pleasant weekend at the lake and claimed to also be going away himself. He didn't add that his briefcase contained the documents for the widow Miller, or that he was heading to Holmes County especially to see her on his own dime.

By the time he had loaded his duffel bag into the trunk and the briefcase on the passenger seat beside him, John was ready to admit that he wasn't going to Holmes County to see a client. He was going to Holmes County to find out if what he felt for Emma was real, or if it had been sympathy for the victim of an arranged marriage.

If he was completely honest, it was also to get out of the city. Those few days in Holmes County had brought him more peace than a day at the beach ever had. The slower pace, the friendly people and of course the appeal of the plain life.

He arrived late on Friday afternoon and, after checking into the guesthouse he had booked online, he was more than anxious to see Emma. It was Friday evening and he knew it would be inappropriate for him to just show up without an appointment, but he couldn't stand the thought of waiting until morning to see how she had been.

Three weeks ago when he left, he had glanced at her in the rearview mirror and promised himself he would never come back. But now he couldn't wait to walk up the stairs onto that porch again. A smile spread on his mouth as he grabbed his keys and headed to his car. Emma might be surprised to see him, but secretly he couldn't help but hope that she would also be very glad.

Would Ruth be there? Would she have told Emma about her plans to leave the community yet?

John navigated the back roads before turning onto the dirt road that led to Emma's house. A smile played on his mouth as he remembered Eli King, and he wondered what the miserable old man had to say for himself when he found out about Emma's wealth.

There was so much he wanted to tell her. He wanted to tell her about the case he was working on, a case he didn't believe in. He wanted to tell her how much he had missed her, and he wanted to tell her how much he had missed Holmes County during the time he had been back in Cleveland. But before he could tell her anything, John wanted to know how she had been. Was she grieving? Did she miss him? Would she be happy to see him?

As the house came into view, John knew there would only be one way to find out.

Chapter Seventeen

An unexpected dinner guest

Emma glanced at the large pot of beef stew on the stove and breathed out a heavy sigh. When was she going to learn that she was only cooking for one, and no longer for a man with a healthy appetite? She wouldn't let the extra stew go to waste; instead, she would freeze it and save herself having to cook on another evening. A knock at the door startled her for just a moment.

Her heart skipped a beat, hoping it would be Ruth. After Ruth's announcement that she would be leaving the community, she hadn't seen her sister again. Granted it had only been a few days, but Emma couldn't help but hope that they would enjoy as many meals together as possible before Ruth set off for her new life in the *Englisch* world. Although Ruth's announcement hadn't come as a shock to her, Emma had to admit to feeling disappointed. When Ruth left she would officially have no one. She knew her sister would never be happy in the Amish world, but she couldn't help but fear that her sister would also never find happiness in the *Englisch* world. What if Ruth left only to learn that the *Englisch* life wasn't what she was looking for? She wouldn't be able to return, and she would have to live her life in regret.

Emma pushed the negative thoughts aside and headed to the front door. With a smile, she opened the door ready to welcome her sister, only to find John Fisher on her porch. Her heart skipped a beat, even as she felt the smile broaden on her face. Over the last few weeks she had tried to convince herself so many times that what she had felt for John was simply a figment of her imagination, the result of all the loss she had suffered.

But looking into his green eyes right now made her realize that it hadn't been her imagination at all.

"John?" Emma asked hesitantly, still unable to believe her eyes.

A teasing smile played on his mouth. "Emma?" John returned in the same unbelieving tone of voice.

"What are you doing here?" Suddenly Emma felt a little self-conscious. If she had known he was coming, she would've made sure not to look like a woman who had spent the day cleaning a *haus*.

John held the briefcase aloft with a shrug. "I bring good news, and access to bank accounts."

Emma's breath caught, she had been hoping for this moment over the last few weeks and now that it was suddenly here, it was all the more surreal somehow.

"You mean I have access to the accounts?"

John nodded. "To every single one of them. Emma Miller, you are as of this moment a very wealthy widow."

Emma shook her head unable to comprehend what he was saying. "You'd best come inside. I've made way too much stew for myself, and I think a little sustenance would go a very long way right about now."

Emma stepped back to let him inside.

"I don't expect you to feed me, Emma," John said with a grin as he stepped into the house.

Emma glanced over her shoulder and smiled at him, "You've traveled all this way, and you come bearing good news, the least I can do is feed you."

John inhaled two plates of stew before Emma made them coffee. Her appetite had disappeared the moment John had stepped into her house again. Regardless of the reason for his visit, Emma couldn't help the overwhelming emotion of joy that flooded her system to see him again. When he hadn't left word at the restaurant, she had thought she might have imagined the connection they had shared. But seeing him again just confirmed what she had felt over those few short days.

After explaining the different bank accounts, surprising her with the life insurance policy, and explaining the technicalities of the checkbooks and checking account, John turned to her with a grin.

"I know we still have a way to go with the deeds, but at least this will allow you to pay off the debt."

Emma shook her head, baffled by everything. The life insurance policy was more generous even than the bank accounts that received the lease payments. "I can't believe David was so well prepared. I wish I could tell him how grateful I am."

"I know, it isn't the case with every will that the widow is taken care of this well," John said, closing the folder and pushing it toward her.

Emma glanced down at the documents before meeting John's questioning look again. "I appreciate you coming all this way to bring me this. I'm sure you could have used a courier."

John's eyes met hers and he tilted his head slightly. "Yes, I could have, but then I wouldn't have had the pleasure of your company or your cooking. Besides, it's Labor Day weekend, and I thought I'd spend the weekend in Holmes County and make the most of the time away from the humdrum of the city."

Before Emma could change her mind a smile lifted the corners of her mouth. "Tomorrow is the annual farmer's market in town, if you'd like to join me?"

A smile slowly tugged up the corners of John's mouth. "I'd like that very much."

Chapter Eighteen

A landlord, a bishop and a few frowns

John had been looking forward to spending the day with Emma all night, but as soon as they drew up at the annual farmer's market, he doubted his decision. As soon as Emma climbed out of his car, he noticed an elderly Amish couple walking by with raised brows. Emma climbed out and joined him without noticing.

"Emma, do you think this is a good idea? I don't want your reputation to be tarnished in any way?" John asked quietly beside her.

"John, if it were any other day I might've been bothered. But it's the farmer's market, and besides, it's not like we're holding hands or staring into each other's eyes." Emma's teasing smile made John's heart skip a beat. What would she do if he told her he wished that they had been holding hands and staring into each other's eyes?

"You're right. So where do we start?" John asked,

glancing at the myriad of stalls that lined the football field.

Emma laughed. "Just where we want, or we could work our way from one side to the other, if you prefer?"

"That sounds like a plan," John said before they fell into step and headed to the left side of the field.

John couldn't believe the variety of arts, crafts and fresh produce that he encountered as they walked through the lines of stalls. There was everything from quilts right down to handmade jams and freshly picked string beans. By the time they reached the last aisle, his tummy was rumbling from all the mouthwatering fare that had taunted him that morning. "Can I interest you in some apple strudel?"

Emma chuckled. "I thought you'd never ask." She seemed different today, as if she was relaxed, and if John was a gambling man he would've bet she felt happy. He couldn't help but wonder whether it was because she was relieved now that she finally had access to pay off her debts, or if it was because of his company. Maybe both?

John bought them each a serving of the strudel, which they ate as they moved on to the next stall. He was surprised to find Ruth standing behind a table covered with beautiful quilts.

"Emma! I was hoping you'd come today." Ruth's eyes turned toward John and widened slightly. "John? It's a surprise to see you back in Holmes County."

John nodded. "I had some things to deliver to your sister and so I thought I'd spend the day."

Ruth's brow rose slightly. "I guess Emma can afford an expensive lawyer to travel from the city to see her."

John felt Emma stiffen beside him and decided not to tolerate Ruth's forwardness and risk her ruining what had been a lovely day so far. "Emma, look. There is Eli King."

He saw the shadows disappear from Emma's expression as she smiled at him. "Come on, John, I have my first check to write."

John didn't know who was more excited to hand Eli a check for six months' rent paid in advance, him or Emma. To see surprise dawn on the miserable man's face must've been the best part of his day.

Just as they turned to inspect the items at the next stall, John bumped into an elderly Amish man. "I'm sorry, please forgive me."

"It's alright," the elderly man said before glancing at Emma. "Emma, how nice to see you out today. Is this *mann* a friend of yours?"

Confused, John turned to Emma who nodded. "*Jah*, Bishop, this is my lawyer. John Fisher, please meet Bishop Lapp."

John expected the Bishop to frown and make it clear that he didn't approve of Emma keeping company with an *Englisch* man, but the bishop rather turned to him with the curious gaze.

"John Fisher? Your father was Peter Fisher, wasn't he?"

John nodded slowly. "He was."

The bishop chuckled softly. "You have his likeness,

recognized it the moment Emma mentioned your name. How is he? It was a sad day when he decided to leave."

John felt a little off balance by the bishop having recognized him, not to mention the reminder that this man had once been their bishop as well. "He passed, eight years ago."

"I'm sorry to hear that, John. Losing a parent is never easy. I know the whole community felt the loss when your *mamm* passed."

John nodded, unsure what to say.

Luckily, Emma filled the silence for him. "John is handling David's will; he has gone to a great deal of trouble to make matters easier for me."

"That's good to hear," the bishop said kindly.

"Please send my regards to Mrs. Lapp and thank her again for the casseroles," Emma said before glancing at John.

"Of course, I will. John, it was good to see you again. Feel free to visit us any time."

John greeted the bishop before he and Emma set off toward the next stall. But as he walked away he couldn't help but glance back over his shoulder at the departing bishop. At the churches he had attended in Cleveland, it was rare for a bishop to remember the name of every person in his congregation. And yet, even after leaving Holmes County fifteen years ago, Bishop Lapp still remembered him and his family. Instead of making John feel unwelcome because he and his father had left the community to become *Englisch*, John had felt welcomed by the leader of their erstwhile community.

Chapter Nineteen

An awkward goodbye

When John and Emma finally reached the last stall at the farmer's market, Emma was sad for the day to end. It wouldn't be appropriate for her to invite John to dinner again, not after he had dined with her the night before. She had thoroughly enjoyed spending the day with him and wasn't looking forward to saying goodbye again.

Last time she had said goodbye she had hoped the affection she felt for John had simply been a figment of her imagination. But now she knew it was real. Just as real as her heart skipping a beat when he looked at her as soon as they climbed back into his car.

"If you don't mind, I was hoping you'd show me where the cemetery is. I want to stop by there and put some flowers on my mother's grave before heading back to Cleveland."

Emma's heart swelled in her chest, it wasn't every man that wanted to place flowers on his mother's grave.

"If you'd like, I can come with. I haven't been there since David's funeral."

"I'd like that very much. Do you know where we can stop for flowers?" John asked as he gunned the engine.

Emma directed him to a florist in town and then they headed out of town to the Amish cemetery. As soon as he climbed out of the car, John turned to Emma with a questioning look. "They are all wooden crosses?"

Emma nodded. For a moment she had forgotten that John hadn't been Amish for a very long time and probably couldn't remember their customs when it came to burials. "We don't believe in expensive tombstones. The soul of those who pass have rejoined with *Gott*; the wooden cross is merely a reminder that for a short while they belonged to us."

"I think my mother's grave is on that side." John pointed to the far side of the cemetery.

Emma nodded, glancing in another direction. "David and my *mamm* are over there."

"Want me to go with you first?" John asked. For a moment Emma considered saying no. It felt wrong asking David to accompany her to her husband's grave, but then she realized that he more than likely didn't want to face his mother's grave on his own.

"I'd appreciate it."

Together they walked through the graves, surrounded by the solemn atmosphere of the graveyard. Neither said a word, both lost in their own thoughts until they reached Bethany's grave.

Emma kneeled and carefully placed the bouquet of fresh flowers before the cross marking her mother's grave. She said a quiet prayer before standing up and moving over to David's.

Here she took longer. John held back and gave her the privacy she needed to say everything she needed to say to David. Emma took a deep breath and whispered the words she wished she could have said in person.

"I'm so sorry I couldn't love you the way you loved me. I think if I'd known how you felt, things might've been different. Thank you for everything. I never expected you to leave me with anything except for the fond memories of our quiet dinners together. I hope you find peace and happiness with *Gott*. Rest now, and trust that I will always keep you in my heart."

She felt the emotions clog her throat and quickly wiped away a tear. Now that she knew how David had felt about her, it was no longer quite as easy to stand beside his grave. She couldn't help but feel guilty that she didn't return his love.

She turned and found John watching her. After swallowing down the emotions, she summoned a smile. "This was harder than I thought it would be."

John nodded. "It usually is."

Together, they moved across the graveyard toward his mother's grave. Just as he had done for her, Emma gave him the privacy he deserved to say a few words to his mother. By the time John joined her side they were both a little overwhelmed.

Quietly, they made their way back to the car, but before John opened the door for her he turned to her and searched her gaze. "You know what I just realized? I just realized we need to cherish every moment that we have with the ones we love, because they can be ripped away without a moment's notice."

Emma nodded and felt her heart swell in her chest. Their eyes met and the connection Emma thought she had imagined before was definitely there again. Only this time it was stronger. Was this what love felt like? Affection? Or was this merely sympathy for a *mann* who had visited his mother's grave for the first time in years?

In her heart she knew the truth. She knew that his words didn't only apply to people they had already lost but in a way for her it applied to the feelings she had for John. They were stronger than any she had ever experienced before, but Emma knew she couldn't act on them. She was recently widowed, and John was an *Englischer*. Regardless of having spent the day together, Emma knew there was no future for them together. She quickly glanced away before clearing her throat. "If you don't mind, I'd like to go home now. I'm quite tired after today."

It was a white lie, but one Emma had to tell to hide her emotions from him. John didn't argue but opened the door for her and then drove her home. This time there was no longing look when he said goodbye. Emma rushed up the porch steps and closed the door before John could see what was in her heart.

Chapter Twenty

A change of pace

The case had been postponed again.

This time not by the prosecutor, but due to Seymour. After the prosecutor had revealed new evidence, Seymour had requested an extension for the trial date in order to prepare his defense.

Things were looking ever bleaker for Seymour's client with each passing day, and John couldn't help but silently be pleased for it.

It had been two months now since he had visited Emma in Holmes County and, although he tried to push the deeds office to finalize transferring the properties into her name, some things just couldn't be rushed.

But that didn't mean he didn't think about her. Something had changed for John on that day at the farmer's market. He wasn't sure what it was but seeing the bishop and spending the day with Emma had made him wish that he was again a part of that community.

He knew it was a foolish thought, especially because his whole life had been lived in Cleveland, but without realizing it John was scaling back on the hours he put in at the firm. Instead of spending every night at the office trying to land a new client, or to put in more billable hours, John headed home at five o'clock all the more often.

None of the partners had commented on John's change of pace, but it was as if the ambition and the drive that had earned John his position as a senior associate within only a few years of joining the firm, had simply vanished.

He would spend his evenings quietly at home reading the Bible and cooking, instead of grabbing the usual take out and watching mindless television. Most nights he would remember Emma and the sad look in her eye when she had turned to him from beside her husband's grave. She might not have loved David Miller, but it was clear that day, that she did have feelings for him. Even if those feelings were simply respect and affection, John couldn't help but for a moment to be jealous of a dead man.

When he was with Emma it was as if he was a different man. He wasn't defending a sociopath, or a drug lord, or hiding the flaws of a corporate shark. He was simply being John Fisher. If he was honest with himself, he liked that person more than the one who walked into a law firm every morning to prove his worth.

While driving home to the city from Holmes County after visiting his mother's grave, John had wondered for the first time whether he could perhaps have a different life. Would he be able to leave the corporate world behind? Would he be able to leave the technology and the luxuries of his *Englisch* life behind? Seeing the bishop had made John realize once again that the decision to leave hadn't been his, and as the Bishop had said, he was welcome to come and visit any time.

John found himself wondering when he would be able to make the time to visit Holmes County again. He wanted to see Emma again, but this time he wouldn't mind stopping by the bishop's home as well.

A phone call from Seymour late that evening brought John back to the present and his reality. His dreams of a different life were foolish when he had responsibilities right here in Cleveland. Seymour and Pascal had given him a chance when no other firm was willing to take on a guy fresh out of law school. Before he could even consider any changes, he owed it to them to see the trial through first.

He kept it to himself that he secretly hoped that their client would be found guilty and did everything Seymour asked of him, but every night before he went to bed, he prayed that justice might prevail.

He also prayed that God would guard Emma and keep her safe.

Chapter Twenty-One

A revelation

Emma's eyes were still swollen from crying after she dropped Ruth off at the bus stop. It had taken her sister a few weeks to tie up all she needed to in order to leave her Amish life behind. The entire time Emma had hoped that Ruth would change her mind.

But she hadn't.

Less than thirty minutes ago she had kissed her sister goodbye and wished her well before Ruth had boarded the bus to Cleveland. Emma had no idea of Ruth's future or immediate plans but had given her sister the balance of her mother's estate with which to start a new life. Since she was in town anyway, she decided to go to the restaurant as she did on most days, instead of heading home where she knew she would only cry the rest of the day away.

As she crossed the road to the restaurant, a man caught her eye in the distance. Her breath caught and for a moment she thought it might be John. When he turned and looked her way her heart sank into her feet realizing it was just another *Englischer* with the same color hair. How long would it take before she no longer had thoughts of John every moment of every day? When the will was finalized? She didn't know the answer, but she did know that she had never enjoyed spending the day with a man more than she had spending the day at the farmer's market with him. That was more than a few weeks ago and yet Emma could still remember every detail of that day.

She hadn't heard from John since and couldn't decide if it was better that way or worse. On the one hand, she was grateful because it gave her time to settle into a new routine without her mother or David to take into consideration. On the other hand, she missed his conversation over dinner almost every night.

She turned and headed into the restaurant where Stephanie and Josh had just finished cleaning the floors. Ever since David had passed, Emma had been waiting to feel like their new boss, but every day when she arrived at the restaurant she couldn't help but dread everything that needed to be done. Stephanie and Josh provided ample support with the administration of the business, but that didn't make the task any more pleasant.

Stephanie greeted her before she followed Josh into the kitchen to make sure everything was ready for the doors to open in an hour. Emma stood in the center of the restaurant and glanced around, feeling the familiar dread settle on her shoulders.

After John's visit she had managed to pay off all the debt David had incurred, and the restaurant was now turning a solid profit. With daily specials thought up by Josh, and Stephanie's sociable personality that encouraged clients to stay little longer and spend more money, the restaurant was doing better than ever before.

This should have been making her happy, but she didn't feel even an ounce of pride. It was hard to admit that something that belonged to her felt like a lead weight pulling her deeper and deeper into a pit of despair.

A thought occurred to her and for a moment a frown creased her brow. She had never considered selling any of David's assets before that moment but glancing around the restaurant now, Emma knew that this was not what she wanted for her life. She didn't want to spend her days waiting tables and ordering supplies for the kitchen. She had only worked at the restaurant because her mother had urged her to at first, and then only because she had married David.

Without her mother or David around to push her into a business that she had no interest in, Emma realized it was her choice whether or not she wanted to keep it. Having just dropped Ruth off, who was chasing her own happiness, Emma decided it was time for her to chase her dreams too.

A small smile formed on her mouth as the dread lifted from her shoulders, simply at the thought of selling the restaurant. For a moment she wished John was there to consult on her decision but realized that part of moving on with her life was making the hard decisions on her own. She headed to the office to think things over. She looked over the financial accounts and tried to come up with what would be a reasonable price for a restaurant in a small town in Holmes County. Before it dawned on her she didn't need the money. It wouldn't be right simply to just walk away from the restaurant, but nor did she need to sell it for an exorbitant amount.

With her decision made she headed to the kitchen where Stephanie and Josh looked at her in surprise as soon she stepped into the kitchen. "Do you have a minute? There is something I need to tell you," Emma asked, feeling hopeful for the first time in months.

Emma told them her plan to sell the restaurant and expected both to be shocked and to beg her not to. Instead, Josh stepped forward with a cocked brow. "Have you decided on a price?"

Emma shrugged. "I have. I'm sure the restaurant is worth much more, but I'd rather sell it than keep it. I know you must think me unfeeling, but that isn't the case."

Josh shook his head. "It's not unfeeling, and it's clear to both me and Stephanie that this restaurant isn't your passion. If you don't mind my saying so. What price are you asking?"

Stephanie turned to her brother with a surprised look. "Josh, what are you thinking?"

Josh didn't answer and waited instead for Emma to answer. Emma named a price and expected him to look shocked, but he simply turned to Stephanie. "With the profits we're turning every month, we could afford to buy the restaurant and to pay off a loan from the bank."

Emma couldn't help but be surprised; she didn't even consider that Stephanie and Josh would be interested in buying the restaurant. "If you're really interested in buying it, I wouldn't expect you to get a loan from the bank. Maybe we can come to an arrangement where you can just pay me off instead."

Stephanie gasped, surprised. "You would do that for us?"

Emma nodded. "I know how hard you work, and I would like nothing better than to know I'm leaving it in your hands."

Josh smiled and stepped toward Emma. "That would be great."

Relieved, Emma smiled and held out her hand. "Then it's a deal. I'm going to work out a payment schedule over a number of months that wouldn't make the payments too steep. I know that some months are harder than others. In those months please don't hesitate to let me know if you can't make the payment, and we can work something out."

"You've just made our day," Josh said before glancing at his sister.

Emma headed back to office from where she could still hear the brother and sister excitedly celebrating. She was both relieved and excited. Not only was she getting rid of the responsibility of the restaurant, but she was handing it over to the very people who would benefit the most.

Chapter Twenty-Two

Date night

John still couldn't seem to find the peace he was searching for in his life. Regardless of the shortened work hours and the wholesome meals he was now cooking for himself, something still didn't feel right. He couldn't stop thinking about Emma, knowing that a future with her was impossible. So he did what any other man would do, he turned to another woman hoping she would make him forget about the one he could never have.

It was a trendy restaurant in an upscale part of town. The type where you didn't even like or understand the art on the walls, but you were nonetheless intimidated by it all. Each table had a candle in the center to create a romantic ambiance, and the table cloths were starched to within an inch of their lives.

Across from him sat a beautiful blonde woman with clear blue eyes and a generous smile. After meeting her at a lawyer's mixer a few weeks ago hosted by his firm, John had finally decided to take her up on her offer to meet for dinner. Allison Beaumont was a shark in the legal world. Her reputation preceded her, just as her beauty was admired by most in the courtroom.

She was attractive, kind and funny; the type of woman John had always liked.

"I hear you're working with Seymour on the Blackman trial. If you win this one, it's going to mean the world for your career."

Usually talk of work and trials would have excited John, but tonight he couldn't even muster the smallest ounce of excitement. "So they say. But enough of work, tell me a bit more about you."

Allison smiled, and John couldn't help but admit that she was even more beautiful in the light of the flickering candle. Although she was a very attractive woman, John didn't feel a modicum of attraction to her.

"What would you like to know? Much like you, my life revolves around the courtroom and my current clients."

John nodded, understanding, because his life hadn't been much different a while ago. "If your life could have revolved around other things, which would you have preferred to include?"

Allison chuckled softly. "Traveling definitely. I'd love to explore the mysteries of the East, or even trek through the jungles of South America."

John smiled, intrigued, or at least trying to be. "That sounds interesting and if you weren't traveling? Would you enjoy cooking? Or a day in the country? Perhaps even a spot of gardening?"

Allison's eyes widened with surprise. "Are you crazy? The closest thing I'll come to the country are the vegetables on my plate. Gardening," she glanced down at her manicured French tips and shook her head. "These nails wouldn't survive. And unfortunately, when it comes to cooking, I much prefer someone else to do the cooking and cleaning leaving me to just enjoy the fruits of their labor."

John kept the smile in place although he knew without a doubt that his dinner was Allison would lead to no more than him asking for the check as soon as it was over. Not because of her aversion to cooking or dirt but because it was clear they were nothing alike.

John caught himself thinking about Emma again and he wondered what she might be up to. Did she think about him at all? It had been weeks since he'd seen her and even though he had a beautiful woman at the table with him, he was thinking about Emma. When would he finally stop reminiscing about the widow he could never love? Or the life he had left more than fifteen years ago?

"John? Is something wrong?" Allison asked reaching for his hand across the table.

John shook his head and retracted his hand. "No, nothing is wrong. I'm just tired. Working on the Blackman trial is catching up with me, I guess."

Through the rest of dinner he kept the conversation light and tried to keep his thoughts in the present, because if he allowed them they would keep drifting back to Emma and her hazel-brown eyes that captivated him every time he went to Holmes County.

Chapter Twenty-Three

Sign on the dotted line

Emma's hand paused over the dotted line of the contract. Was she doing the right thing? Without having to manage the restaurant, what would she do all day? She was only twenty-two years old and couldn't spend the rest of her life doing nothing.

Fear suddenly raced down her spine. Was she giving up on life before it had even really begun? She pushed the thought aside and knew it was ridiculous. She might be young, but she had already been married, lost her mother and her husband and more recently her sister.

Although Ruth wasn't dead, Emma knew the chances of hearing from her sister again were slim. Apart from receiving a message through Stephanie that she had found a place to stay and landed work as an admin clerk in Cleveland, Emma didn't know if she would ever see her sister again.

The lawyer cleared his throat and Emma's gaze

darted up to meet his. "I'm sorry; this is just a big decision for me."

"Are you having second thoughts?" Josh asked hesitantly beside her.

They were in the lawyer's office to sign the agreement of sale as well as the contract for the installments of the repayment. Emma shook her head and summoned a smile. "Not at all. I know selling the restaurant is the right thing to do."

Without further pause she signed on the dotted line before sliding the document over to Stephanie and Josh to sign. As soon as all the required signatures were on the documents, Emma felt the weight lift off her shoulders. Tomorrow she wouldn't have to worry about the restaurant's takings or the orders that needed to be placed.

In fact, she would never have to worry about that, or unhappy and impatient patrons ever again. A smile lifted the corners of her mouth as she glanced at the new owners of her restaurant. "Congratulations. I wish you the best of success for the future."

"*Denke*, Emma," Stephanie said gratefully.

"I don't think you realize it, but Stephanie and I have always dreamed of owning our own restaurant. You've just made our dreams come true."

Emma felt her heart clench in her chest and wished she knew what her dream was. Once, long ago she had dreamed of having a husband and a family to care for. Now she had nothing. She only had the money David had left her and realized that although wealth could ease worry, it didn't keep you warm at night.

She left the lawyer's office and headed home. As soon as she stepped into the kitchen she knew she needed something to keep her busy. On a whim she decided to bake a chocolate cake to celebrate the sale of the restaurant. She knew the restaurant had been David's dream, but it had never been hers.

As she pulled the freshly baked cake out of the oven and the aroma of chocolate filled the air, she remembered the first time John had come to see her. He had all but inhaled the cake before hesitantly asking for more.

She missed him every day and prayed for his happiness every night. She hadn't heard from him in too long and she was beginning to realize that she shouldn't count on hearing from him again in the future. Perhaps their day at the farmer's market had been their final farewell. Once the will was finalized and the deeds transferred into her name, he could send the documents to her by courier. The chances of ever seeing John again were less than slim. She slid the cakes onto the cooling rack just as a knock at her door caught her attention.

The bishop's wife, Mrs. Lapp, stood on the threshold with a kind smile. "Mrs. Lapp, what a nice surprise."

Deliveries of casseroles and pity food had stopped a month before already, and Emma couldn't think of a single reason for the bishop's wife having come to see her.

"Emma dear, I'm so glad you're home. I have a proposition for you," Mrs. Lapp announced with an air of formality.

Emma welcomed her inside and showed her to the kitchen where she poured them each a cup of tea. Once they were settled on the porch, Emma turned to Mrs.

Lapp with a questioning look. "What proposition is it that you have for me?"

"You know the farm stall, the one on your way to town?" Mrs. Lapp asked and waited for Emma to nod before she continued. "Ever since I can remember, I've been baking for them. Cakes, pies, cookies…"

"Really?" Emma asked, surprised. "I never knew it was anyone from our community doing the baking."

The bishop's wife chuckled softly. "I suppose I didn't make a fuss of it. I don't expect anyone knows that I was baking for them."

Emma nodded, wondering where this conversation was going. "From what I've heard, it's some of the best baked goods around."

"That's why I'm here, Emma. My arthritis has been playing up over these last couple of months. I simply can't keep up with the orders anymore. I know your *mamm* used to tell me what an avid baker you are, and I was wondering whether you would you be interested in taking it over for me?"

Emma's jaw dropped slightly. She had always enjoyed baking but had never given any thought to selling her baked goods.

"I'm not sure my baking is half as good as yours."

"Of course it is. I've tasted your baking on many occasions. That's why I came to you. I know you still have your hands full with a restaurant and David's will, but I was hoping you might be interested."

"Actually, I just sold the restaurant today," Emma said with a smile. She still couldn't believe she no longer had the weight or responsibility of the restaurant weighing on her shoulders.

Mrs. Lapp clapped her hands together with glee. "Then it's perfect; you have more than enough time to bake for the farm stall instead."

Emma thought for a moment, giving pause to wonder whether she wanted to bake for a living, before a smile slowly spread across her mouth. In the past she had only baked on special occasions and knew that she would enjoy it if she had a reason to bake every day. "Are you sure?"

Mrs. Lapp smiled with a nod. "Definitely. The Lord works in mysterious ways, and this morning when I woke up with my hands aching, you came to mind. It seems you have just closed the door on an old chapter, and you have now opened a window on a new one."

Emma couldn't help but smile at the sound of that. Indeed, she had just closed the door on the life she hadn't chosen for herself and was now starting to realize what it meant when you grabbed opportunities with both hands, to find your own happiness.

Chapter Twenty-Four

Courtrooms & history lessons

After a long day in court, John was eager to get home. The Blackman court case had finally started, and the more he was faced with the prosecutor's evidence, the more John realized he was sitting on the wrong side of the courtroom.

It was early days yet in the court case, and Seymour and John still had to present the jury with a defense, but John didn't think their defense would be strong enough. Not because they hadn't prepared enough, but because the prosecutor's evidence was painting a very true likeness of the accused. A teacher who abused his power in order to sell drugs to students, and who had hired a hit man when things didn't go quite his way.

He decided to walk home to clear his mind instead of taking a cab as he usually would on the days when he was in court. While he walked home he couldn't help but wonder if he had gone into the wrong arm of the law. Perhaps if he had become a prosecutor, he wouldn't have felt like a fraud protecting the scum of the earth. Perhaps, even becoming a police officer would have been better than going into private law practice.

He wanted to see Blackman go down; he wanted to see him found guilty. More than anything, John wanted to see Blackman pay for the crimes he committed by sitting in jail for a very long time. Of course he couldn't voice this opinion to Seymour or Pascal, as it would be a breach of his oath to defend the firm's client.

By the time John stepped into his house, he felt emotionally drained and couldn't help but detest the man he had become.

Just like he had known that things would not work out with Allison, but not for lack of trying on her side. If it had been Allison's choice, their dinner would have led to more, a lot more than John had been prepared for. But he had greeted her with a friendly kiss on the cheek and headed home. He had waited a few days before he called her and told her that it would be best if they kept their relationship professional. John had heard the disappointment in her voice but hadn't let that change his mind.

He wouldn't admit that it was simply because she wasn't Emma; rather, he convinced himself that she just wasn't the right fit. After nuking a microwave meal, John grabbed a bottle of water and headed to the living room. He flopped down on the sofa and flicked the television on, hoping for some mindless entertainment to take his mind off his day. After taking the first bite of the tasteless meal, he couldn't help but wish for a meal of Emma's cooking again. Or, if he was honest, her conversation.

His heart skipped a beat when a person dressed in plainclothes moved across the television screen before a presenter appeared and began his address. After just a few seconds John didn't even notice the tasteless food he was shoveling into his mouth. Coincidentally the program on air was about the Amish heritage and how the first settlers had decided to draw up the first *ordnung*.

He listened, intrigued, to how his forefathers had decided to create a community in which technology and politics wouldn't be allowed to infiltrate their lives. A community where faith, family and community would be held sacred and cherished for years to come.

Even after his meal was finished, John kept watching as he learned more about the Amish history and how generations of Amish people had stood up against controversy, politicians and public scrutiny. And yet regardless of all that, they remained true to their roots. He was honored, and humbled to know that this was his heritage. His forefathers were pioneers and John now more than ever regretted that his father had taken the decision out of his hands for him to stay.

He set the microwave dinner aside and wondered how different his life would have been if he had stayed. Would he have courted Emma had he still been Amish? Would he have yearned for an *Englisch* life like Ruth did?

Or would he have been grateful for the opportunity to live a plain life with people who still valued character over the wealth? His thoughts turned back to the

Blackman case and he knew that if he had been Amish he wouldn't even have considered defending someone who was so clearly guilty of the charges he was facing.

It was a bitter pill to swallow, to know that he was defending a man who didn't deserve a defense. He headed to bed and opened his bible to find and read a passage about judgment. After reading the passage a few times over, John realized that it wasn't his place to judge Blackman, but that the ultimate judgment would be passed when Blackman reached St. Peter's Gates. Every man deserved a fair defense, and John wouldn't judge Blackman for his actions, but neither could he stand the thought of defending him.

Chapter Twenty-Five

A new beginning

Emma stopped the buggy outside the farm stall and took a deep breath. Although she had never doubted her ability to bake, it was a different matter when she was being paid for it. She was grateful to the bishop's wife for setting her up with this opportunity and only hoped that the proprietor of the farm stall was happy with her baking.

She grabbed the chocolate cake and an apple pie and made a note to herself to get more cake tins if she was going to continue baking for the farm stall, before she headed inside. She had been inside the farm stall only a few times before and had always admired the variety of homemade jams, cookies and crafts. Instead of browsing through the products as she usually would, Emma headed straight to the checkout counter where a handsome man was ringing up the purchases for an *Englisch* woman.

"Be with you in a moment."

Emma smiled, surprised to see that he was also Amish. She had never realized the farm stall belonged to an Amish man before now. As soon as he was finished with his customer he came out around the counter and smiled at her before holding out his hand.

"I'm Abram Yoder; here, let me help you with those."

He took the tins from her and Emma smiled. "I'm Emma Miller. I've got some more in the buggy if you'd like them."

Abram was tall—taller than David was—and he had warm brown eyes. His hair was black, reminding Emma of the night sky. He was a very attractive man, and not much older than Emma.

"Of course I'd like them. Mrs. Lapp couldn't stop talking about how *wunderbaar* your baking was. I'm very glad she found you to replace her." Abram smiled at her in a way that made her realize he was more than interested in just her baking.

She shifted uncomfortably in place. "Let me just go and fetch them."

She headed outside, wondering why Abram made her uncomfortable before reminding herself that she was recently widowed. As soon as the thought occurred to her it was replaced by the memory of how she had felt when John looked at her in exactly the same way. She hadn't felt uncomfortable beneath John's gaze; instead, she had felt her heart swell and her cheeks warm.

Emma carried the rest of the cakes inside and, after settling on a fair price, Abram paid her for her trouble. Although Emma was now a very rich woman, she couldn't help but feel proud to have earned her own money for the first time in her life, without her mother or David's help.

She had enjoyed baking every single one of those cakes, pies and tarts for the farm stall and in turn had been paid for it handsomely. It was a good feeling to know that, regardless of the wealth she had inherited from her husband, she was finally earning a keep for herself.

"Would you like to join me for *kaffe*? I was just about to go and make some for myself," Abram offered with a gracious smile.

Emma shook her head quickly. "*Nee, denke*. I have a few other chores I need to do today. Would next Friday be all right for the next delivery?"

Abram nodded. "I'm sure that'll be fine. If it's not, you can just give me your address and I'll stop by to let you know when these are finished."

Emma's heart suddenly raced. Why did she feel uncomfortable by the prospect of giving this man her address? It was clear that he wasn't from their community, or she would've known him. He must be from the community on the other side of town. Although he was Amish, Emma didn't feel comfortable giving him her address.

"That won't be necessary; I'll stop by Monday afternoon to check in. *Denke*, again."

Emma rushed back to the buggy and picked up the reins before snapping them and turning to the horse. "Step on."

On the way home her thoughts drifted to John once

again. She hadn't seen him in a long time and yet she still thought of him almost every day. She wondered if Ruth had contacted him, and if they might now be dating. It was foolish to be jealous of her sister, when she didn't even know whether Ruth and John had made contact with each other.

When she finally arrived at the house she had once shared with David, a smile lifted the corners of her mouth knowing she had finally made it a home. The front yard look cheerful with the winter shrubs and Emma couldn't wait to see what it would look like in spring when she could plant more flowering shrubs. Although the vegetable garden only boasted winter squashes, Emma enjoyed knowing that she had planted them herself.

She was starting to build a life for herself, a life which brought her happiness even if she had to admit it was lonely.

Chapter Twenty-Six

A welcome break

A combination of things had led John to packing a suitcase and heading back to Holmes County. Firstly, he had arrived in court on Tuesday morning only to find that the judge had been admitted to hospital due to an allergic reaction and that the case would therefore be postponed until the following Monday.

Secondly, he had returned to the office only to find out that the deeds had been returned by the deeds office, and everything had been transferred into Emma's name.

The final straw had been the email from the human resources department alerting him that failure to take the leave days due to him would most certainly result in him losing them at the end of the month.

John read through the email and was startled to find that he had eighty-nine days' leave accumulated over the last few years. He sat back in his chair with a heavy sigh, realizing that except for the odd day of sick leave he had taken when he had the flu, he hadn't once taken a holiday or made use of his leave. A quick phone call later and a subsequent white lie to Seymour, saw John put in for a few days leave, citing personal reasons, before he headed home to pack.

He arrived in Holmes County early afternoon and stopped by the restaurant in the hopes of surprising Emma by his arrival. Only Emma wasn't there. Stephanie recognized him immediately and quickly asked if he was looking for Emma or a meal.

With a wry smile John admitted to the first. He was surprised to find out that Stephanie and her brother had bought the restaurant from Emma. For a moment he had feared that Emma had moved away to move on with her life without contacting him. Stephanie, however, quickly set the record straight.

"She is still living in the same place; she just didn't want the restaurant anymore." Stephanie's brow furrowed before she continued. "Were you looking for her with regards to David's will?"

John nodded, not wanting to add that he was looking for her also because he wanted to see her again. A short while later he was on his way to Emma's house, his heart racing in his chest at the thought of seeing her again.

He had a valid reason for going to see her, as he needed to hand over the deed documents, but John also knew that wasn't the only reason he wanted to see her. He wasn't lying when he said he needed a few personal days. He wanted to take a few days to explore what he felt for Emma, and the confusing feelings he had with regards to his Amish heritage. While spending these few days in Holmes County, John hoped to pay a visit to the bishop as well.

He stopped in front of Emma's house, and noticed that the front door was open, but the screen door was closed. After knocking a few times, Emma still hadn't come to the door. Taking a chance, John opened the screen door and slipped inside, heading to the kitchen where he could hear someone moving around.

She turned to him in surprise when he cleared his throat, looking to him to be about as cute as a button. She had flour on her nose, and her hands were covered with it too even as a smile spread across her mouth. John's heart swelled in his chest just a fleeting moment before he had the sensation tantamount to a punch to the gut.

It slammed him like a bullet between the eyes, the realization that this was where he wanted to be. The law, Cleveland, and his luxurious lifestyle no longer appealed to him. It was the plain life, the beautiful yet plain woman who stood before him, and the slower pace that now appealed to him and made him doubt all the decisions he had ever made in his life.

"John? What are you doing here?" Emma chuckled softly, glancing down at the state she was in. "If I had known you were coming, I would have cleaned up this mess, and myself."

John shook his head. "You look perfect just as you are. I bought the deed documents; I thought delivering them in person might be a good idea."

Emma's face brightened. "Really, they've all been

transferred? Wait, just give me a moment to clean up this mess and I'll make us some coffee and then you can tell me all about it."

John stood aside as she quickly dealt with the flour and the batter she was mixing, before she made them each a cup of coffee. They headed outside to sit on the porch.

It was Emma who spoke first. "Would you like to stay for dinner?" She smiled and shook her head as if in response to her own invitation. "If you're here this early in the afternoon, you probably want to head back tonight."

John shook his head. "This time there is no rush. I took a few personal days to work through some matters." John could see the question burning in her eyes, but she did not ask him what he meant.

"Then you'll stay for dinner?" Emma asked hopefully.

John smiled with a nod. He might have come to Holmes County to deal with his own personal issues, but he couldn't turn down an evening with Emma. "Will Ruth be joining us?"

A sad look crossed Emma's face. "No, she won't. She left about a month ago."

John couldn't help but be surprised. Although he had known that Ruth had planned on leaving the community, he hadn't thought she would go through with it, at least not this soon. "Do you know where she went?"

Emma held his gaze for a moment before she nodded. "Cleveland. Hasn't she made contact with you?"

John shook his head. Had Ruth made contact with

him, he would've helped her where he could, but he knew for certain that nothing more would have come of it. Regardless of Ruth's interest in him, John had no interest in being any more than a kind friend to her. "How have you been doing?"

Emma shrugged. "I've sold the restaurant; I realized it wasn't what I wanted to do with my life. I'm now baking for the farm stall, which kind of explains all the flour, doesn't it?"

John chuckled. "I'm sure they are very grateful. I've never tasted a chocolate cake as good as yours."

With a late afternoon sun skirting over the horizon painting the sky in beautiful natural hues, John cherished the moment. He didn't know when he would be able to sit with Emma again in contented silence and he also recognized that he had a lot of decisions to make over this week.

He knew without a doubt that none of those decisions would be easy.

Chapter Twenty-Seven

Honesty is the best policy

Emma was overjoyed that John was back in Holmes County. Although she wouldn't admit it to him, she had hoped he would return one day with the deed documents in hand. She had safely stowed the title deeds in the safety deposit box at the local bank, knowing with some measure of relief that David's will was finally dealt with.

When John had surprised her that evening and they had shared a meal alone together, they had both remained relatively quiet for most of the evening. For Emma it was a matter of doubting her own feelings. Whenever she saw John, the feelings were stronger than before, and every time he left it became all the harder for her to forget him.

She had prayed for guidance and yet she was still waiting for God to send a sign on how she should deal with his return. She didn't see him the day before and was secretly grateful for having a little time to herself to mull over the feelings she was struggling to understand.

But when he stopped by that morning to invite her to lunch later in the afternoon, Emma couldn't resist. She couldn't stand the thought of saying goodbye again, but she knew she would regret it if she didn't spend time with him while he was there. He had mentioned personal issues he needed to work through, and although Emma had no idea what he meant by that, she felt flattered that he had made the time to spend some with her as well.

He had swung by early afternoon to pick her up, and instead of going to the restaurant that Emma used to own, they had driven to the next town over, and dined at a little Italian restaurant that Emma had only ever heard about.

She was grateful that she wouldn't have Stephanie and Josh gawk at them for most of the afternoon but couldn't help but wonder if it was appropriate for her to join an *Englisch mann* for lunch in a strange town. Emma knew that she was getting very close to being inappropriate, but she pushed the thought aside.

Emma had never been to an Italian restaurant before and was truly amazed at the variety on the menu. John ordered lasagna and Emma opted for the cannelloni.

They spoke a little about what they had been up to since they had last seen each other, and Emma explained her decision to sell the restaurant to him as well as her choice to bake for the farm stall. John encouraged her and praised her for taking a brave step toward a new life.

Glowing in his praise, Emma smiled as she reached for a glass of water. "And you? Have you taken any brave steps in the last few months?" Emma asked in a teasing tone of voice. But the look that came into John's eyes made her realize that he didn't take the question quite as lightly as she had intended.

"Actually, I'm trying to take a few brave steps this week." He let out a heavy sigh before shaking his head and returning Emma's gaze. "Coming back to Holmes County all those months ago made me remember the life I'd left behind. I'm starting to wonder if I would have left had my father not made the decision for me."

Emma felt her heart skip a beat, even as hope bloomed in her chest. Did this mean that John was considering becoming Amish again? She didn't voice her question, though, and when John changed the subject she knew he wasn't ready to answer it just yet. When they eventually arrived home, Emma was surprised to find a basket of fruit on her porch.

Curious, John followed her up the porch steps, where Emma retrieved a handwritten note from the basket. The note was short, but it caused her heart to clench in her chest with sadness.

My dearest Emma,

I hope this note finds you well. I didn't tell you this earlier, but I left Holmes County with the bishop's permission on an extended holiday. I have made my final decision, and I hope you understand that I won't be coming back.

I've also sent a basket of fruit to the bishop, to notify him of this decision. I know what this decision will mean for us, and I know with certainty that I will be shunned.

I trust you can forgive me, and I wish you every happiness for the future and all it might hold for you. Just as I'd hoped, I am happy, Emma. This is who I was meant to be. I know it's hard for you to understand and I hope that one day you will, but right now I know you must be devastated. Especially after losing David and Mother.

Please pray for me and please take care of yourself.

Your loving sister,
Ruth

"I thought the decision had already been made?" John asked in surprise from beside her.

Emma nodded. "So did I, but now I know she'll never come back. Even if she wants to, the bishop won't let her."

Emma felt the tears start to form in her eyes and she quickly looked away. She didn't want John to see her like this, but she couldn't hide her disappointment or the sadness of knowing she wouldn't see her sister again.

She felt John's hand rest on her shoulder followed by the soft words he whispered behind her. "I remember my mother once said, everything happens for a reason. We might not understand the reason, but in those times we have to fall back on our faith."

Emma turned around and searched John's gaze. It was the words of an Amish woman, she recognized as much because her mother said the same many times when she was young. But to hear them now from the *Englisch mann* she was refusing to fall in love with, made her wonder if meeting John hadn't happened for a reason as well.

Chapter Twenty-Eight

The eyes hide nothing

John returned to Cleveland with a very heavy heart the following week. This time he had no doubt that he wanted to stay, but unfortunately it wasn't as simple as that. He had responsibilities in Cleveland. Over and above all that, he had to decide whether or not he was willing to leave his *Englisch* life before he committed to an Amish life. He couldn't stand the thought of leaving Emma but was placated in the knowledge that the community would take care of her, just as they had taken care of him and his father after his mother had passed away.

He fell right back into the routine of going to work and coming home alone every evening. The case was moving along swiftly, and although matters were looking all the bleaker for his client, John wasn't nervous as he would certainly have been before now. Instead, he was secretly hoping that matters might begin to look even worse.

One afternoon, after court, he bumped into Allison on the steps of the courthouse.

She smiled at him brightly. "John, what a pleasure to see you again. I see the Blackman case is almost winding to a close. I am sure you have high hopes for the final verdict?"

John summoned a smile, the best he could possibly muster. The last thing he needed was for Pascal and Seymour to find out that he wasn't rooting for an innocent verdict. "That remains to be seen. How have you been, Allison?"

Allison flicked her blonde hair over her shoulder and smiled up at John. "I've been well. I would have been better if I had a dinner with you to look forward to again."

The flirtatious smile did not go by unnoticed, and John was not surprised by the realization that he could not summon any interest in looking forward to a dinner with her again. "This case is keeping me wrapped up at all hours."

Allison nodded. "I get that. Some cases are just like that."

John took another step down, ready to say goodbye when Allison stopped him with a touch to his arm. "John, when I said dinner, I didn't necessarily mean a date. It was clear from our last date that you weren't interested. It could just be dinner as friends?"

John chuckled wryly. "Was it that obvious?"

Allison shook her head with a softened gaze. "No, it

was obvious that you were troubled. I don't know what's going on with your life, or what troubles you are facing, but I want you to know that if you need a shoulder you can always call me."

John couldn't help but be taken aback. He had been battling with his feelings for Emma along with the troubling emotions with regards to his Amish heritage for the past few months, and he had assumed that he done a good job of hiding it. But looking at Allison now, he realized he hadn't done as good a job of it at all, especially if a complete stranger could've picked up that he was troubled. "I'm fine, really; it's just been a busy few months. As soon as this case is dealt with I'll be able to breathe again."

Allison nodded but she held his gaze. "The offer stands. I'll see you again, good luck with the Blackman trial."

John watched her walk away and wished not for the first time that he was back in Holmes County. That he was back where he felt comfortable, welcome and at home. The courtroom had always been his playground, and now it was nothing but a gruesome reminder of the horrors that people were able to commit.

Instead of going home as he had planned, John stopped by a florist shop and decided to do something he had never done before.

He sent flowers to a woman.

A woman who he knew deserved flowers, a woman who brightened his day although she was more than two hours' drive away.

Chapter Twenty-Nine

The final verdict

"We the jury, after taking into consideration all the evidence presented to us, find the accused, Adam Blackman, guilty of all charges."

Cheers erupted throughout the courtroom as justice had prevailed and another monster would spend the rest of his life in jail to consider the crimes he had committed against society. On the side of the courtroom occupied by the defendants, no celebration was seen to be had.

Seymour cursed under his breath even as Pascal slammed his fist on the table. Secretly, John was cheering along with the rest of the courtroom. They had just lost one of their biggest cases yet. Seymour had just let down a close family friend, but John couldn't be disappointed. Not when it meant that Blackman would spend the rest of his life in jail, paying for the life he had ordered to be taken and the crimes he had committed whilst dealing drugs to children.

He followed the partners out of the courthouse and joined them in the black town car summoned to ferry them back to the law firm. The ride up in the elevator was quiet, solemn even, as if someone had very recently passed away. John couldn't manage to summon even the slightest feeling of disappointment. This had been the verdict he had been hoping for, the verdict he had been praying for, for months. He knew that Seymour would likely be nearing a breakdown of some sort, and Pascal would probably go on a drinking binge tonight, but he didn't care.

As soon as the elevator doors opened to their floor, Seymour turned to him with a murderous expression, "John, my office, now!"

John nodded as Seymour stomped off in the direction of his corner office.

He took a deep breath and followed behind as Seymour waved his assistant away when she rushed at him with a barrage of messages. As soon as John stepped inside the office, he closed the door behind him.

Seymour was standing before the windows, Pascal was already pouring himself a drink, and John simply waited patiently to hear the reason for having been summoned. After what seemed like forever Seymour turned around, his jaw clenched as his eyes bored into John's.

"Congratulations, John. I gave you one of the biggest cases of your career, and you dropped the ball. I don't know what's been going on with you, but the fire that was in your eyes on the day I hired you, seems to have lost its spark." Seymour sighed impatiently as he moved a step closer to John.

"This was an open and shut case. But no, you were too busy mucking around with the Miller widow to pay any attention to this case. Now that the Miller will has been finalized, I expect I can once again count on your complete cooperation again. No more slacking off and heading home at five o'clock. Clock watchers have never been welcomed at this firm. Do you hear me?"

John nodded. A few years ago he would've been terrified, shaking in his shoes right now, but he didn't feel the least bit threatened. Was it because he didn't value his job as much as he had back then, or was it because his career was no longer the only thing of importance in his life?

"I'm giving you one last chance to prove that I was wise in hiring you." Seymour turned around and grabbed a file from his table before handing it to John. "Roman Cortez has to appear in court next week on charges of money laundering. I assured him that you will be able to make the charges disappear before he needs to appear in court. I don't care how you do it, just do it."

John felt unease bloom in his chest as he paged through the file. Roman Cortez was guilty of money laundering but that wasn't the full extent of his guilt. Roman Cortez was one of the biggest drug dealers in Cleveland. The money he was accused of laundering was drug money.

Bile rose in John's throat at the thought of defending yet another lowlife. He closed the file and looked directly at Seymour who was still glaring at him. Looking into Seymour's eyes brought a bible phrase to mind. One that had been sticking with John ever since he read it a couple of weeks ago during the week he had spent in Holmes County.

Matthew 7:14: Because strait is the gate, and narrow is the way, which leadeth unto life, and few there be that find it.

A smile slowly spread across John's face, knowing that this was the sign he had been waiting for. This was the sign he needed to make that final decision. The decision to change his life and allow himself to be the man he wanted to be. He had an easy life until now. Wealth, women, the admiration of his colleagues. He had become the man he had always wanted to be, only to realize it wasn't who he wanted to be at all.

Not a ruthless shark in a world where compassion was lost, and crime was celebrated. He carefully moved to the desk and lay the folder down. "Seymour," John turned to meet the eyes of the man who had once promised to make him a famous lawyer, "I quit."

Seymour's face turned red and John would not have been in the least surprised if steam had started rising from his ears in that very moment. "What?"

John shrugged and suppressed the smile that threatened to break out across his face. "I quit. You don't have to worry about other offers, or making me a better offer, or trying to convince me that this is the right law firm for me. I'm done with private law. I quit."

"Pascal!" Seymour shouted across the room. "Do you hear this?"

John sighed, turning to Pascal. "Don't even bother, Pascal; you won't be able to change my mind. I'm done. Thank you for the opportunity and for taking a chance on me. I'll always appreciate that you believed in me."

Seymour kept shouting about John being a nitwit, selfish, and something about him having an emotional breakdown. John waited until he had finished his rant before he answered all the accusations in a very calm voice. "I went into law because I wanted to protect the victims. Yes, I might have been young and naïve, and I might even have been wearing rose-colored glasses. But since then, I've learned that the world isn't just black and white. I know now that there are various shades of gray in between. But with all respect, I'm done chasing after money and ignoring integrity and what is right. I need to be able to look myself in the mirror and know that the client I'm defending deserves my defense. There was no defense for what Blackman did. And as for Cortez, I'm sorry I can't defend a man like that. I'll clear my desk by the end of the day and make sure all my files are handed over to one of the associates."

John didn't wait for either man to answer; instead, he turned and walked out of the office knowing that he had just burned a bridge it had taken him many strained years to build.

Chapter Thirty

~❧~

A new resident

Emma couldn't help but wonder if she had just done the right thing by turning down Abram's invitation to dinner yet again. She knew an invitation to dinner would be perfectly appropriate, given that it had been eight months since she had lost David, but Emma simply couldn't muster any excitement at the prospect of being courted by Abram Yoder.

She knew that she would have many prospects of courting opportunities in the future, especially since she was a young widow, but that didn't bother her in the least. Besides, there was little use in being courted by a *mann* she didn't love. Emma had been married to a *mann* she didn't love and had promised herself over David's grave that she would never spend time with a *mann* she didn't love ever again. Her thoughts drifted to John, who she hadn't seen in the last two months. Ever since David's will had been finalized, she hadn't heard so much as a word from him apart from the flowers he had sent over a month before.

Emma had been in town taking care of some chores when she had stopped by the restaurant to catch up with Stephanie, only to find a beautiful bouquet of roses on her porch when she returned home. For a moment she had thought that they had been from Ruth and had found herself eager to hear all about her sister's new life. But when she had picked up the note, her heart had skipped a beat to read John's name at the bottom.

The message had been simple.

Flowers for the woman who brightens up my day.
May they brighten yours,

John

Emma still didn't know what to make of the flowers he had sent her, especially since she hadn't heard from him again, but she still thought about him almost every day. Especially today, after turning Abram down. As she turned the buggy onto the dirt road leading to the house that passed the home in which she had grown up, a frown creased Emma's brow.

In the driveway stood a U-Haul. Her heart simply shattered all over again, knowing that neither her mother nor her sister would ever be coming back. She knew the house couldn't stand vacant forever, and that the owners probably needed the lease income, but it still hurt to know that someone else was moving into her childhood room. Someone else would be cooking in her mother's kitchen. And someone else would be sitting by the fireplace that her father used to stoke for them in winter when she was a little girl.

Regret washed over her for a moment as she considered whether or not she should have bought the property herself when she was able. She quickly pushed the thought away, knowing that it would have been a bad investment. Not only did she not need another property, she certainly did not need the strain of another tenant to worry about. The house might have been her childhood home, but the house she was currently leasing from Eli King had become her home.

She slowed the horse, eager to get a look at the new residents of the community, when a man suddenly emerged out the front door. Her heart skipped a beat and she blinked a few times, certain that her eyes were simply fooling her. It was probably just a combination of a hard day, little sleep, and all she had faced that year, Emma tried to convince herself when she opened her eyes again.

But the vision before her didn't change. The man currently walking toward the buggy was John Fisher. He was wearing plain clothes along with a foolish grin as he approached her.

Emma climbed out of the buggy, stunned and speechless all at once to see John there. "John? What are you doing here? With a U-Haul, no less?"

John shrugged as a smile dawned on his face. "Well, I was hoping to be settled in before I saw you, but I'm not sad that you stopped by." John glanced back at the house before meeting her questioning gaze again. "It took me eight months, but I finally realized that although my father might well have taken away my choice fifteen years ago to remain Amish, I could nevertheless still make my own choice now. This time I know it is the right choice for me. When I was here two months ago, I met with the bishop. He agreed to allow me a proving period to decide whether or not I would like to stay in the community again. I know I took my time to decide, but I wanted to be sure. Last week, something happened that made me realize that I want to be nowhere else than right here in Holmes County where I belong."

Emma's heart was bouncing in her chest even as she struggled to comprehend everything John was saying. He was staying, he was becoming Amish, and he was back.

She shook her head, her mouth slightly agape, not knowing how to respond when, John chuckled and continued.

"The bishop was kind enough to agree to let me do legal work for the community. It won't be at city rates, but this time I'll be working for a purpose and not the bottom line."

"I'm happy for you, John, I'm really happy for you," Emma said, unable to believe the trick that fate had just played on her. A few moments ago she had wondered if she had done the right thing by turning Abram Yoder down, and now a future with John Fisher might well be a possibility.

"It's really good to see you, Emma, but I've got to get

back inside. These loading people are always in a rush. Can I stop by later?" John asked hopefully.

A smile blossomed on Emma's face, like the roses he had sent her a while ago. "I'd like that very much, John."

Chapter Thirty-One

~∞~

Wood stoves are complicated things

John watched as Emma drove away and he felt his heart soar. He had hoped that he would be settled in before meeting Emma. He was planning on keeping a low profile and surprising her with an invitation to dinner before asking if he could court her. But fate had other plans.

He couldn't even disagree with fate—the best part of his day so far between the packing the moving, and hauling all the furniture inside, had been seeing Emma.

He had sold most of his furniture back in Cleveland and had only brought two couches, a dining room table and his bed, along with a few groceries and linens, with him to Holmes County. When the moving guy finally left, John sat down on the couch in his living room and sighed, suddenly realizing the extent of what he had done.

He had no drapes, no proper food, and he didn't even have any form of transportation. During his proving period, the bishop offered to personally teach him everything about being Amish again, and suddenly John hoped that would include learning how to care for a horse and drive a buggy.

A smile curved his mouth at the thought of one day taking Emma on a buggy ride.

He started unpacking the boxes and then made his bed before heading around the house to find a pile of wood. After lugging the wood inside, he shoved it into the wood stove and lit the fire. Only once the stove was hot, did John realize he didn't even own a kettle that didn't work without electricity.

Through the kitchen window he could see Emma's house in the distance and a smile curved his mouth. Was that not what neighbors were for?

With a skip in his step, he headed toward Emma's house. He knocked and a short while later she opened the door. "John, this is a surprise. Done already?"

John shook his head with a chuckle. "Not at all. But I just realized I have nothing to boil water in, and the few groceries I do have consist of microwave dinners, microwave popcorn and not much else. And then there's the problem of operating the wood stove. Who knew it could be so complicated?"

When Emma's laughter bubbled freely, John couldn't help but smile. "You think this is very funny, don't you?"

Emma shrugged and opened the door for him to step inside. "*Nee*, not at all. I just find it very entertaining how the *Englischers* think we have such an easy life, but they don't realize just how hard it can be to simply brew a cup of *kaffe*. Would you like some?"

John nodded gratefully as he followed her into the kitchen. Today he had started his new life, but as he followed her into her kitchen, he couldn't help but wonder if he had just opened the door on the possibility of romance as well. Of course that had been his wish ever since he decided on coming back to Holmes County, but to see her joy in having him return was worth more than winning all the court cases in the world.

"Thank you, Emma, I have so much to tell you. About my meeting with the bishop, the proving period, and everything I have to learn before I can be baptized. It's quite intimidating actually, but I have faith that I have a friend in Holmes County."

Emma smiled at him warmly, and John felt his heart swell. "Of course I'll help. Hanging drapes, cleaning, and making a *haus* a home has never been a *mann*'s job, after all."

John chuckled softly as he took a seat at the table. "Is making dinner also a man's job around here?"

Emma shook her head. "John Fisher, are you trying to get an invitation for dinner out of me?"

Between the eight months since he had met Emma and now, he couldn't help but appreciate the significant change she had undergone. Gone was the shy widow who could barely look him in the eye, and in her stead he was faced with a confident woman who had clearly made a home for herself and was freely enjoying his company. He no longer doubted whether or not she had also felt the connection so long ago, and instead looked forward to exploring it with her in future. Perhaps even flirting with her a little.

"Perhaps, would it work?"

Emma thought for a moment before she finally met his gaze again. "If you don't mind bean stew and beet-root salad, you're more than welcome. Welcome to Holmes County, John."

Chapter Thirty-Two

Like a flower in bloom, her heart opens to love

Over the first few weeks following John's arrival in Holmes County, Emma felt herself warm to him all the more. Without the barrier of their backgrounds and David's death hanging over them, Emma found herself falling in love for the first time in her life.

She knew the bishop and his wife approved of her association with John, as they had often driven to church together and the bishop always welcomed them and wished them a wonderful day, as if realizing that they shared a Sunday lunch almost every week.

It was a welcome feeling to know that Emma could finally act on her feelings and not feel hemmed in by her mother's expectations or dreading the moment that John would go back to Cleveland. He took to Amish life like a duck to water. She had expected him to struggle at first, especially given that it had been fifteen years since he left his Amish life for the *Englisch* world, but everything came back to him, almost as if riding a bicycle.

They didn't see each other every day but on most days John would stop by. They would have coffee, lunch, or sometimes even dinner and every time she saw him, she would learn something new about John that she appreciated.

She had come to realize that John was a man who cared deeply for animals. And although some men might be intimidated by the sheer size of a horse, the horses simply loved John. He hated chickens, and only kept them around because most Amish people did. One day he had confided in her that it might be un-Amish of him not to have a chicken coop. Emma knew in her heart though that he would never have the heart to slaughter one of his hens.

He had set up one of the rooms in his home as a makeshift office for his small law practice. Since his arrival in Holmes County he had not only helped a few of the community with legal matters, but he had also made sure that every single person in the community now had an actionable will in the event of the inevitable occurring.

John had stopped by that morning to collect her delivery of cakes and pies for the farm stall, as he sometimes did if he had a chore in town, when a police cruiser pulled into her yard. Emma felt cold sweat bead on her face at the site of the policeman climbing out of the car. The last time a policeman had paid a visit to her house, it was to tell her that David was dead. Relief washed over her as she glanced at John standing beside her. At least she wouldn't lose another person she loved today. She suddenly thought of Ruth and dread filled her, wondering if something might have happened to her beloved sister.

"Good morning, are you Mrs. Miller?" the policeman asked in a formal matter.

"I am," Emma admitted quietly.

"I have information with regards to your late husband's death, Mrs. Miller. If you like, we could go sit down somewhere where we can talk privately," the policeman said, glancing at John.

Emma turned to John before turning back to the policeman. "If you don't mind, Officer, this is my lawyer. I'd prefer if he was present."

Emma saw the appreciation in John's face before they turned and headed into the house. Once everyone was seated at the kitchen table, the police officer didn't hesitate to begin.

"Mrs. Miller, I'm not sure if you are aware of any of this, but what I'm about to tell you might be surprising, to say the least."

Emma nodded and took a deep breath. "Officer, I didn't know my husband very long before he passed away. So I'm sure whatever you are about to tell me will be surprising, but I assure you that I can handle it." Emma couldn't help but feel proud of herself. She was no longer the victim of loss, and now felt in control of her life for the first time.

"Our investigation reveals that Mr. David Miller started a restaurant in a small town in Missouri with a partner over ten years ago. At first the restaurant struggled financially and Mr. Miller's partner bailed when things got a little hard. Mr. Miller managed to turn the restaurant around to earn a steady profit in just a few years. Three years ago he was made a generous offer for the original restaurant along with franchising rights. When his partner got word of this offer, he started hounding Mr. Miller for a share of the profit."

"But he wouldn't be due any profit, because he wasn't part of the restaurant anymore. You know if there is a legal contract binding him to this restaurant?"

Emma's head bobbed between the police officer and John, confused by the legal jargon they had just used. In essence, she knew he was asking whether or not she had to pay this man.

"No, there had been no contracts of any sort between Mr. Miller and his previous partner. It seemed that because Mr. Miller refused to pay him a share of the profits, his partner decided he might give David a fright by running him over and that David would then pay up. Or at least that's what he is testifying to. We took him into custody a few days ago. An eyewitness reported seeing him at the scene. The paint on his vehicle matched the scrapes of paint we found on the buggy. Without a doubt, this is the man that killed David Miller."

Emma gasped, surprised that David had been going through a challenging time himself and didn't care to share it with her. She was grateful that his murderer was finally convicted but couldn't help but wish that David had confided in her. Before the time came for the police officer to leave, he assured her that she didn't owe David's ex-partner anything.

Emma couldn't help but be relieved, because now with David's will and his murder finally behind her, she could finally move on with her life. She turned to John and prayed that he would remain a part of her new life as well.

Chapter Thirty-Three

Declaration of love

On a rainy Sunday afternoon, John sat by the fire and glanced out the window at the dreary landscape. It was hard to believe that he had been in Holmes County for almost four months already. He only had two months left of his proving period before he could be baptized into the church. So much had happened in the last four months, but John still knew without a doubt that he wanted to be nowhere else. The day he was baptized would be the best day of his life.

The best part about his move to Holmes County was the legal work he was doing. It felt good to know that he was helping people instead of protecting criminals. His relationship with Emma had also grown. Although neither had mentioned their feelings or admitted their affection for one another, it was clear to John that she felt the same.

John had planned to tell Emma his feelings after his

baptism, but suddenly he didn't want to wait any longer. It had been almost a year since they first met, almost a year of denying his feelings and pretending that they didn't exist. John was ready to tell Emma how he felt. He was ready to ask her to spend the rest of her life with him. He was ready to commit the rest of his life to her.

For a man who had never thought he would enjoy picket fences, chicken coops, and happily ever afters, this was quite a revelation. A smile lifted the corners of John's mouth as he grabbed his coat and braved the rain to walk the short distance over to Emma's house. He knocked on the door and waited for her to answer, realizing he was completely soaked. But he didn't care. In that moment nothing mattered more than the woman opening the door and the concern on her face.

"John? Is something wrong?" Emma asked, instantly concerned.

John shook his head as a slow smile started to form. "Emma, I don't want to wait any longer. I know it's raining, and you're probably busy, and it's Sunday afternoon and not an appropriate time to really visit, but I can't wait another minute."

Emma frowned, confusion clear in her gaze. "John, what on earth you talking about?"

She glanced at the soaked coat and shook her head. "Come inside out of the rain."

John smiled but he didn't move. "No, not before I have said what I've come to say. Emma Miller, since the first moment you opened the door to me, I knew you would change my life. That day I felt like a horrible man, attracted to a widow who was still grieving her husband. I felt the connection that first week, and I kept coming back trying to convince myself it wasn't real. But it's real, Emma. Nothing in my life has ever been more real. I think I should've realized what I felt for you when I insisted on handling David's will myself. Usually, a paralegal would be assigned to deal with such matters, but I wouldn't hand you over. Because that would mean not seeing you again. Over these last few months, I've not only learned who I really want to be, but I've learned with whom I want to share my life. I don't know if it's appropriate, or if a certain time should pass, or if you even feel the same way." John chuckled softly. "But I think it's time that I told you that I'm in love with you. I'd like to court you. And I'd like you to know right now that I plan to marry you."

Chapter Thirty-Four

Hearts, roses and happy ever afters

Emma's heart skipped a beat even as tears began streaming over her face. John was right, for the last year she had denied her feelings, needing to play the part of the grieving widow although she had barely known her husband. He had stood by her side during the toughest time of her life, and he had made her realize what it means to really love someone.

He had shown her that people can change. That even if you're caught up in a life that you knew would only blacken your soul, you could get out of it.

He was the bravest man she had ever known, to leave everything he had achieved in the *Englisch* world to become Amish again and to reconnect with his roots. He was kind, generous, smart and funny, and Emma had fallen in love with him without even wanting to.

Over these last few weeks they had not only become good friends, he had also become the person she wanted to spend her days with. On the days she didn't see him, she missed him, although he only lived a stone's throw away.

She knew she would always cherish the memories she had of David and that she would always cherish knowing how much David had loved her and knowing the lengths her mother had taken to secure her marriage, even though she still felt guilty because she didn't love David in the same way. But if there was one thing that she could take away from her marriage to David, it was that, if you love someone you had to do it with your whole heart.

David had gone through so much to make her fall in love with him and he hadn't succeeded. But she had fallen in love with John without any pressure or scheming from anyone.

She knew without a doubt that she loved the man before her more than life itself. She wanted to share the rest of her life with him and raise a family with him.

She had only been widowed a year ago but knew that she was ready to get married again. There would be practicalities such as John's baptism and the bishop's permission to deal with first, but Emma knew that fate wouldn't have put them together on this journey enduring over a year, if it hadn't been intended for them to spend the rest of their lives cherishing the love they shared. She stepped forward and framed John's face with her hands.

He was wet, but she didn't mind. She searched his green eyes and smiled. "John, I've been afraid of the feelings I had for you since the first moment I met you, but you're right, the time has come for us to be honest. I love you, too."

Emma dropped her hands and stepped back, waiting for his reaction. John didn't say a single word. He reached for her hand and pressed a kiss to the back of it before looking into her eyes again.

"That's really good news, but I have a little bit of bad news for you. I don't know how to be an Amish husband," John said with a teasing smile.

Emma laughed, feeling all the sadness, fear and anxiousness of the last year disappear. "It's easy; you just have to love me."

Epilogue

Three years later...

John sat at the kitchen table on a cloudy Tuesday evening. He dropped his head into his hands and sighed heavily. He glanced down at the number of ledgers and receipts before him and simply couldn't find the answer he had been hoping for.

Emma turned away from the stove and glanced at her husband with concern. "John? What's wrong?"

John shook his head as he met her gaze with despair in his eyes. "Emma, it doesn't matter which way I work these numbers, the practice just isn't making money."

Emma chuckled and shook her head. "John, you didn't start this practice to make money. You started it up to help people. And I can't even count the number of people you've helped over these last few years. That's the real number that matters, not whatever is in your ledgers. Besides, why are you worrying about the bottom line? You married a wealthy widow."

John laughed and closed the books before turning to Emma with a handsome smile. Although they didn't live a luxurious lifestyle, Emma's investments and lease incomes allowed for them not to have to be worried if John's practice didn't turn a profit.

"Oh, but did I tell you, she isn't just wealthy? She's also beautiful, an expert baker, a wonderful wife, and did I tell you that she's a magnificent *Mamm*?"

Emma felt her heart swell as it always did when she looked at her husband. Even three years after the wedding, she still couldn't believe how fate had blessed her with such a wonderful man. For a time in her life she had thought she had no future. She had been faced with a mountain of debt, her mother's passing, and a sister ready to leave the community, only to be blessed with a man who had made all her dreams come true.

She couldn't be happier with the life she had been blessed with and wished her sister had found the same happiness. She heard from Ruth once a year on her birthday. From the last letter she had learned that Ruth had found a wonderful man who she was now dating, and that she had found a good job in a department store. She was happy for her sister but often wondered if Ruth regretted her decision to leave.

She and John still visited their mothers' graves, as well as David's, once a year, and often Emma would thank David and her mother for scheming behind her back. If they hadn't schemed to wed her off so elaborately, she would never have met John.

Besides, John would never have realized that he wanted to return to his Amish roots. It had taken her a long while, but Emma now finally understood that everything did indeed happen for a reason.

If fate ever threw another curveball in her direction, she knew without a doubt that she would accept it with open hands, because sometimes those curveballs might just bring you the greatest blessings of all.

A little girl ran into the kitchen, brown curls tumbled down her back as she looked up at Emma with her father's green eyes. "*Mamm*! The chicken laid an egg!"

John groaned beside her. "Does that mean I have to take her into the chicken coop again?"

Emma nodded with a smile. "I have to finish up dinner and keep an eye on David. He's still fast asleep in his crib."

Some things never change, Emma thought to herself as John followed Bethany outside. She still loved her husband more than anything in the world and, even after three years, he still didn't like chickens. Whereas their little girl was already showing a great interest in the chickens.

While they headed out to collect another egg, Emma closed her eyes and silently thanked the Lord for her blessings, something she did numerous times every day.

Because every blessing was to be cherished; no one knew better than Emma that they could be ripped away in the blink of an eye.

* * * * *

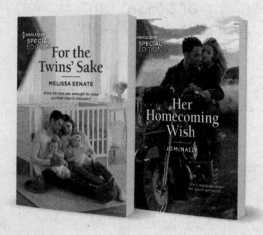

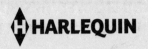

Love Harlequin romance?

DISCOVER.

Be the first to find out about promotions,
news and exclusive content!

Facebook.com/HarlequinBooks

Twitter.com/HarlequinBooks

Instagram.com/HarlequinBooks

Pinterest.com/HarlequinBooks

ReaderService.com

EXPLORE.

Sign up for the Harlequin e-newsletter and
download a free book from any series at
TryHarlequin.com

CONNECT.

Join our Harlequin community to
share your thoughts and connect
with other romance readers!
Facebook.com/groups/HarlequinConnection

Get 4 **FREE REWARDS!**

We'll send you 2 FREE Books plus 2 FREE Mystery Gifts.

Love Inspired books feature uplifting stories where faith helps guide you through life's challenges and discover the promise of a new beginning.

FREE Value Over $20

YES! Please send me 2 FREE Love Inspired Romance novels and my 2 FREE mystery gifts (gifts are worth about $10 retail). After receiving them, if I don't wish to receive any more books, I can return the shipping statement marked "cancel." If I don't cancel, I will receive 6 brand-new novels every month and be billed just $5.24 each for the regular-print edition or $5.99 each for the larger-print edition in the U.S., or $5.74 each for the regular-print edition or $6.24 each for the larger-print edition in Canada. That's a savings of at least 13% off the cover price. It's quite a bargain! Shipping and handling is just 50¢ per book in the U.S. and $1.25 per book in Canada.* I understand that accepting the 2 free books and gifts places me under no obligation to buy anything. I can always return a shipment and cancel at any time. The free books and gifts are mine to keep no matter what I decide.

Choose one: ☐ **Love Inspired Romance Regular-Print** (105/305 IDN GNWC) ☐ **Love Inspired Romance Larger-Print** (122/322 IDN GNWC)

Name (please print)

Address   Apt. #

City   State/Province   Zip/Postal Code

Email: Please check this box ☐ if you would like to receive newsletters and promotional emails from Harlequin Enterprises ULC and its affiliates. You can unsubscribe anytime.

Mail to the **Reader Service:**
IN U.S.A.: P.O. Box 1341, Buffalo, NY 14240-8531
IN CANADA: P.O. Box 603, Fort Erie, Ontario L2A 5X3

Want to try 2 free books from another series? Call 1-800-873-8635 or visit www.ReaderService.com.

---

*Terms and prices subject to change without notice. Prices do not include sales taxes, which will be charged (if applicable) based on your state or country of residence. Canadian residents will be charged applicable taxes. Offer not valid in Quebec. This offer is limited to one order per household. Books received may not be as shown. Not valid for current subscribers to Love Inspired Romance books. All orders subject to approval. Credit or debit balances in a customer's account(s) may be offset by any other outstanding balance owed by or to the customer. Please allow 4 to 6 weeks for delivery. Offer available while quantities last.

Your Privacy—Your information is being collected by Harlequin Enterprises ULC, operating as Reader Service. For a complete summary of the information we collect, how we use this information and to whom it is disclosed, please visit our privacy notice located at corporate.harlequin.com/privacy-notice. From time to time we may also exchange your personal information with reputable third parties. If you wish to opt out of this sharing of your personal information, please visit readerservice.com/consumerchoice or call 1-800-873-8635. **Notice to California Residents**—Under California law, you have specific rights to control and access your data. For more information on these rights and how to exercise them, visit corporate.harlequin.com/california-privacy.   LI20R2